Cross Roads:
Pick a Path

Janaath Vijayaseelan

Copyright © 2015 Janaath Vijayaseelan

All rights reserved.

ISBN: 978-1-329-48251-7

DEDICATION

To my family and friends, who have stuck with me from the beginning of my cross roads.

CONTENTS

1	A Beginning To The End	Pg 11
2	A Walk Down Memory Lane	Pg 16
3	About Time	Pg 35
4	Good Things Come and Go	Pg 41
5	A Tragic Beginning	Pg 47
6	Life Had Other Plans	Pg 52
7	Change is Good?	Pg 58
8	A Welcomed Challenge	Pg 65
9	A Wild Start	Pg 72
10	Let The Games Begin	Pg 86
11	Hostage	Pg 92
12	Making Amends	Pg 110
13	To Fall In and Out of Love	Pg 127
14	Boils Over	Pg 134
15	Tables Turn, Bridges Burn	Pg 154
16	The Collapse	Pg 167
17	Commencement	Pg 187

Preface: Rough Times

When we walk through the paths of life, we come across many roads. With every road comes another cross road. Cross roads that will present you with gifts and glory. Lest we forget, no life is a fairy tale, because every trip of success can quickly turn into a series of unfortunate events. Such is the case of a twenty-seven year old software engineer, Arrun Durai living in Toronto, Canada. Arrun being an individual who lost both his parents to a brutal murder at the age of one, actually managed to live a pleasing lifestyle thanks to a Sarah Gellis; a single mother raising six orphaned children, and of them included Arrun. Well at least until Arrun stumbled into the pit that resulted in a chain of events that he least expected.

In recent days Arrun sits in a dark room, secluded from the world, and the people who were once his life. Crowded with the dense smoke of marijuana, accompanied by the burning sensation of alcohol, all in hopes of forgetting what once was, what she was. Hasini Ravichandran, the girl that walked into his life and altered it forever, only to suddenly part ways in their journey. She left behind a boundless breach within his soul. What bad is there to say of an angel, and that she sincerely was; a beauty that stays posted to your eyes. There is no consumption of drugs or alcohol that ever gives him the peaceful rest he once had. Instead he is endlessly reminded of her smile that kept him going, her eyes that showed a reflection of the complete person he was, her voice he would willingly sit and listen to without complaints. Nothing can help him forget, but to him it is the only way to reminisce in the great times they shared. In contrast to the one incident that made everything collapse.

❖

The time, 2:34am and not content with his daily dose Arrun decided to meet up with his routine dealer, who lives approximately two blocks away from his condo. What he did not know is that his next test of life awaited him, one that is going to lead him to a place where he will have to embark on a journey like none before. A journey that will show him the true colours of what life has to bring.

Unlike every other day in the criminally active city, this night presented itself with the presence of a man who is portrayed as a god to the criminal underworld, Marona Duranji. Only the privileged know of how a man from Chennai, India became one of the most feared dons of the 21st century. Though standing at a mighty six feet three inches in height, with a large build may have something to do with it. Marona at the age of fifty-six is the definition of fear in present times. Hey maybe old, but there is no one, local or of higher authority who has the courage to break him. His ventures in drug trafficking, extortion, kidnapping, prostitution, assassinations, and the business world have led him to pursue a life drenched in cash. Though for a moment of this night, it seemed as if the empire would finally come tumbling down.

Similar to every other day of the past three months, Arrun met up with Remone. The twenty-seven year old henchman of Marona who usually handles the small marijuana deals with the locals. Arrun has been off work for sometime now, has been low on cash. He has been increasing in debt as well, which eventually led to a small dispute with Remone. The small argument eventually started catching the attention of the others around. One of them being Marona, who did not actually seem to show much care. Though something was not right; as Arrun began looking around in humiliation he spotted one of the henchmen standing in the near distance pulling out his pistol, and setting aim towards Marona. Without any hesitation, Arrun rushed towards the henchman tackling him to the ground, receiving a bullet to his right shoulder, one that was meant for Marona. As Arrun laid on the floor breathing heavily looking up at the night sky, occupied with the glow of the stars he knew there is something coming his way. He was ready for it.

Janaath Vijayaseelan

Part 1: Good Things Don't Last

Chapter 1 - A Beginning To The End

July 11 1986 was the day a woman by the name of Sarah Gellis, changed my life forever. Sarah, as she desired to be called was twenty-five when she adopted me. I was not the only one she saved from a life of emptiness; Benny, Mahat, and Asha were all brought into the family at the same time as myself. A year later we were fortunate to have the addition of Rohini and Thiru. A year younger than the rest of us, and they both are without doubt the most bothersome twins you will ever meet; though I still love them with every passing moment my heart beats. Yes we were all orphans, but we never suffered the need to be upset. Brought over from India, she gave us all a better shot at life, raising us in a Western society. Though Sarah was young, and a single mother, she filled the void better than anyone possibly could.

Sarah herself was the product of a single mother, an extremely wealthy single mother at that. When her mother passed away in the year of 1984, she was left with a bulk sum of money, and she had the ability to spend her money on anything she desired. Which raises the question, why didn't she go out and enjoy all that money for her own pleasure?

Especially seeing how it would be a reasonable thing to do at twenty-five. I never paused to question her because there was always something strangely remarkable about her. She had enough money to enjoy a luxurious lifestyle, but she did not want that. Although we all lived under one roof, she wanted us to be brought up as friends over a conventional sibling relationship. My siblings and I all grew up knowing her beliefs were not customary at all, but that is what made her amazing.

She was a complete role model and teacher to the six of us, which is why it was difficult when we lost her at the age of forty-nine on July 16, 2010. She was a strong woman, but sometimes even strongest fall preyed to the devil that is cancer. Times were hard, but it becomes a bit easier when you are one amongst a group of people that were raised by a tough, independent woman. Leaving us with a place to call home, education to live, and knowledge of life, she opened the door to our future.

~

A year passed, and with time wounds healed. We grew accustomed to life without Sarah. There and now her absence remained strong at the back of our mind. Time turns, and things eventually took a turn for the better. During the span of the year we were urgently in need of a diamond in the rough. A few months after the passing of Sarah, Rohini met Akil. Akil, like myself is a software engineer, and truly the spark the entire family needed. I always knew she would be the one that falls in love first amongst the six of us, but she delivered a shock when she announced their marriage only after a year of meeting one another.

I still remember the day she told us like it was yesterday. She called us all into the living room, and alongside Akil she screamed, "We're getting married!" Only God knows how annoyingly loud she was. With Asha joining in, the both of them were soon jumping in circles of joy. In that moment, I was truly more worried about them knocking down the TV in excitement. Putting my feelings aside, I walked over to congratulate Akil; I did not forget to warn him of what he is in for. When Rohini finally began to settle down I stepped towards her, and gave her a hug. Then asked her, "Is this what you truly want," her smile said it all; you could actually tell that she found love. I was never a believer of eternal love, though being raised by a woman that lived life without a partner may have something to do with it. As everyone stood around the living room congratulating the soon to be wedded, I stood curiously wondering whether I would ever stand as ecstatic as Rohini and Akil were in that moment.

"Champagne, Champagne, Champagne", the chanting came from Benny, Mahat, and Thiru. I remembered then of the bottle of Cristal Champagne sitting in my room collecting dust from my trip to France a month ago. Running up the spiral stairs I turned into my room; I had no clue of where the bottle was sitting. While digging through all the junk I brought over from my recent travels, I found the bottle sitting under a pair of my boxers; I will probably keep that part from the rest of them though. When I walked back into the living Benny, Mahat, and Thiru all had the glasses ready with a smile on their face, as if they knew I had it. I wasn't surprised; those three were always the sneaky ones. Standing in a circle, pouring champagne, I thought it maybe the appropriate time to make a toast.

"We all knew it would be Rohini to first find love, and Akil like I said good luck dealing with this one. Jokes aside, I know that I speak on behalf of us all when we wish for a long and healthy life for the both of you.

Together. We maybe all adopted, and refer to one another as friends, but what an amazing feeling it is to have family you can treat as friends. Rohini if Sarah were here with us today, she would be incredibly proud of the beautiful woman you've become. Akil, if Sarah were with us she'd be pleased to bring in another son to the family. Akil, you are now one of us, and if you ever need help I want you to know that your family will always be here for you."

❖

As my eyes opened the pain was obvious, but where I was seemed rather vague. At first my vision felt a bit blurred, but as it became clearer, it was very noticeable that I was actually in a dark abandoned warehouse; must have been a big factory or something. Looking out the window to my left I realized that it was an abandoned warehouse that I have driven by a numerous amount of times. That is when I heard voices. Nearly twenty men stood a few meters apart from the table I assume they had left me on, after being stitched and bandaged. Over their heads, I could see the man that shot me, chained and beaten to the pulp. It was rather obvious that he will not live to see another day. Against a metal beam leaned a shattered mirror with dried blood, and it hit me that I have been so lost in thoughts that I forgot how I used to look. The man in the reflection with a beard and fairly long hair could not be me, but it was. We constantly evolve, and how we adjust to it determines whether you climb higher, or plunge gently. For me, it was time to adapt to my surroundings, like I once used to.

I walked towards the group of men, and I saw Remone's holstered handgun at his waist, and when I took ownership of his gun all eyes were on me. In that moment, I did not pay attention to the men in disbelief, or the ones preparing to fire at me. My focus was purely on the target alone. I stepped towards the man that shot me; I brought the gun towards his head, and pulled the trigger. As the bullet gored through his skull, I hoped for change. It was something poetic; I have lost people, but it was something new to be the person taking away ones existence. There on the floor laid the body of a dead man, one of whom I will never know the name of. Taking turn towards the astonished audience I stood a cold blood killer, and stepping before me was Marona himself. I wasn't that stunted in height myself, but even at six feet in height I had to slightly tilt my head to look the man in the eye.

"You are coming with us to Tamil Nadu." he said with his dreading voice.

I didn't need to say a word. It is almost as if he knew that I would come. Maybe he could see the slash in my soul; after all he was the devil. As he took off with a smirk on his face, the henchmen started to make their way towards me. Two of them walked right by me and carried the body away. I stood there without a care in the world of killing a man, and Remone stepped towards me. "Welcome to the family," he said.

Family, it's funny that the importance of family has not stricken me in sometime now. At one point in my life it was the only thing I lived for, I have not even considered much of why I pushed my family away, even through their constant attempts to talk sense into me. It maybe because I do not have the love I once had to allow people into my life, or it is simply because a lone walk in life sometimes the more favorable option.

Chapter 2 – A Walk Down Memory Lane

On the morning of May 26th, 2011 I woke up to what was arguably the worst hangover of my life. It was also the day before Rohini and Akil's wedding. I have the impression that it was just a few months ago; we were in our living room, making a toast to the newly engaged couple. I guess they must have really been in a rush to get hitched. At times, I do believe Rohini is always in a rush with things, and to be honest I actually would not be surprised if she makes me an uncle in a few months. She is always in a rush to do things, but I knew that she considered everything repeatedly a million times over before committing to a decision. So I was confident that her decision to get married would not have come without a long thought process.

Rolling around in my bed I turned towards the right lamp desk where my sunglasses were sitting. Everything that happened last night is still a blur, but looking out my resort window at the view of the beautiful blue sea, I knew it must have been a crazy night. Although the wedding came soon, I am extremely glad that Rohini and Akil came to the decision of having it in the Dominican Republic. I could probably stick around the hotel room in my boxers for the rest of the day with this headache, but I am not prepared to waste a day in paradise. You would think being twenty-five years old would make me a more organized individual, but I like keeping things a mess; my kind of neat.

My hangover is definitely getting the best of me; at this point I don't give a single care of what I wear. I saw my black basketball shorts and a black t-shirt lying on my bed from yesterday, so I think it is best just wearing those for now. After all, the cute girls are not going to be up at seven in the morning. Honestly, I don't even know what I was doing awake right now. Heading over to the washroom, I needed some urgent attention. My body was asking me to take care of my mandatory human needs as soon as possible; and when I did, my word, it was heavenly. After washing my hands, it felt great brushing my teeth, getting rid of that nasty morning taste after a night of drinking.

A lot of people I have drank with in the past have told me that a shot of alcohol helps cure hangovers in the morning, so hey why not drink down the sample of whisky in the mini fridge. I wasn't an alcoholic or anything, but when I drank, I drank! It only took me a few minutes to get back on my feet again. My immediate reaction was to call, and check where my three idiot brothers were. Asha was probably asleep, and Rohini is most likely dealing with wedding stress. Getting those goofs to pick up their phone is probably going to be extremely hard. They were probably in their rooms asleep, or in the beds of some random girls. Either way I probably should not disturb them; heading over to get some breakfast seemed like a more reasonable plan.

Grabbing my pack of Belmont cigarettes and zippo lighter I made my way out the door. Right outside the door was a maid; I smiled and warned her, "Good luck in there." I could tell she was not looking forward to what she was about to see. To ease her pain I slipped her a twenty-dollar bill. Her reaction made it seem as if she can face the biggest army if they were all crowded in that one room.

Walking out the elevator I can see the heavenly enlarged glass doors leading to paradise. Making my way through the doors I was welcomed by the tall palm trees, morning risers, and the glorifying sun sitting over the horizon of the beautiful water.

Wandering through the courtyard I came across many friendly faces, smiles and morning compliments from everyone. Continuing along the path and over the small bridge I can see Mahat sleeping near the pool. We must have been around here sometime last night; at least I was able to make it to my bed. I was struck with an amusing thought. What if I were to push him into the pool? He would probably be upset, but I could care less because it would be hilarious. As I walked quietly towards him I start to wonder why I'm even trying to be quiet, the guy is out cold. So instead of walking quietly towards him, I rushed to him, and smashed Mahat with a dynamic kick to his ass. His reaction was priceless, he was not pleased, and that was clearly visible by the look on his face. He got out the pool, and walked by me with a dirty look; he grumbled. "Not cool bro, not cool at all."

To me it was hilarious, and as I watched him walking back towards to the hotel doors I got the remaining laughs out of my system. Placing a smoke between my lips I used my zippo to light it up, and continued making my way towards the outdoor breakfast buffet.

There were already a few families sitting at the tables eating breakfast over conversation. I wasn't all that hungry, but some coffee would be extremely helpful right now. After grabbing my cup of coffee I decided to take a seat at the nearby bar. Throwing my smoke in the distance, I took a seat on the bar stool; making a concerted effort to remember the events of last night as I took steady sips from my cup. I should have probably asked Mahat if he remembered anything instead of pushing him into the pool, it was completely worth it though. After a fifteen-minute interval a gorgeous woman came and sat next to me, she seemed a tad bit familiar. I don't think she even acknowledged the fact that I was sitting next to her; either that or she didn't even care.

I am the worst when it comes to speaking to women; I never knew how to start a conversation with them. It caught my attention that she was eating breakfast over at the bar and not at the table like the other folks, but she did not seem like much of a morning drinker. Building some courage I managed to ask her why she was eating breakfast alone at the bar, though her facial expression clearly asked me to mind my own business. I became increasingly curious, and it must be the remaining alcohol in my system but I managed to ask her if we've met before.

"You mean to say that you don't remember me? You don't remember bumping into me last night, knocking down not only my luggage, but me too! How does one not remember being shirtless running down the hallway dancing, and yelling to Tamil songs at 2am? Clearly you were drunk, but you could have had the courtesy to help me up! Asshole."

I just gazed at her with a blank look; I did not recall anything she said, but it was starting to come back to me. I love the music I've grown listening to, the ones popular among Western society, but I loved Tamil music to another extent. I used it as a way of staying connected to my inherited culture. To be honest, all I really took from what she said was that she knew whatever I was singing was Tamil, so she must be of similar background! Without thinking twice, I asked. "Are you Tamil?"

"Seriously all that and that's what you think of saying to me?" she asked, as her anger began to build up.

"What else were you expecting for me to say." I questioned; I actually wanted to be nice, but I did not know what she was expecting from me.

"Uhm how about an apology!" She shouted.

"Right, I am extremely sorry for whatever I did last night." I replied; hoping it was enough to ease her upset state of mind.

"Apology not accepted, now would you let me eat my breakfast peacefully?" She continued.

She didn't seem excited to have me around; she was pretty obnoxious though. Well taking into account the fact that I actually did apologize, and she couldn't accept it. It was probably my queue to leave, but I still wanted to know if she was Tamil. She seemed a bit too fair skinned to be Tamil, but she knew the language of the song I was supposedly dancing to last night. Giving it another shot can't really do much more damage, so once again I asked if she were Tamil.

"Seriously, who are you man? Can't you just leave me alone? If it actually matters that much to you yes, yes I am Tamil! Are you satisfied now? I'm expecting my friend soon, and I'd really appreciate it if your

hideous face wasn't around when she gets here."

I turned to the mirror sitting under the shelves of alcohol and took a look at myself. I always thought I was a handsome guy, and the guy in the mirror thought the same. Silly girl, she probably doesn't have any taste.

"Bitch," I whispered.

"Excuse me, did you say something?" She asked; I'm pretty sure she caught me mumbling.

"Nope, not a word ma'am! I'll be on my way now." I replied; I should probably get going. Wouldn't want to end up leaving the bar with a slap.

Just as I was looking to get up from my seat I saw Rohini walking towards me, waving her hand. So I waved back and remained seated while the gorgeous, but horrifying girl sat next to me, giving me the look of death. With much excitement, Rohini looks towards me and says. "So you've already met my friend?" It took a moment for it to sink in, but it seems that the girls' friend is none other than my very own sister; oh the coincidence is amusing.

"Hasini, meet my brother Arrun." Introduced Rohini.

"This is your brother?" She asked gently.

"Yeah, Arrun is the really quiet, reserved one out of the six of us. Also my favorite," continued Rohini.

"Arrun, this is my best friend; I roomed with her throughout my time at university." said Rohini. Rohini had mentioned the name Hasini a few times, but I've never even seen a picture of her. I wanted to turn to Hasini, and laugh, but I have already started off with a bad impression.

"Ahh I see, I see. She seems to be a very kind person." I said, trying my best to hold in the burst of laughter.

This time around I was not the one with the blank look on my face, Hasini was completely left in shock. She could not believe that she sat there insulting her best friend's brother the entire time. With a smirk on my face, I looked at Rohini and said, "You probably have lots to catch up on, so I'll leave you to it." Walking towards the hotel doors I turned to take a glance at Hasini, she still stared at me from a distance with an embarrassed face. She was a beautiful girl, and there is no denying that, but there was something more to her. Something I could not figure out, and I liked the urge from within, wanting to know more.

~

The wedding was tomorrow, and after a long day of preparations all of us were able to sit at a table full of family, and friends for dinner. Our seating was already pre-arranged. It was actually quite weird, but I was assigned a seat next to Hasini. I was preparing myself for some more boldness to come my way, seeing how she doesn't really like me. Once we sat down for our meals I did not speak a word to Hasini, it was actually a tad bit more awkward than expected. Sitting across from me were the soon to be wed, to my right Hasini, and to my left was Benny. Benny was the family "Playboy" he always managed to smooth talk the ladies. Majority times he doesn't even leave girls for the rest of us to talk to. A brief moment after we sat down he began nudging me, he wanted to sit next to Hasini after seeing how beautiful she was. With a deadly cut eye look, I turned towards him and let him know that I saw her first. While glancing up towards Rohini, I was delivered a wink. I was getting a weird vibe that Rohini may have sat me next to Hasini on purpose; she knows how much difficulty I have talking to women on my own.

After some time the dinner was about to commence, I felt a drop by my foot; looking down, I saw a note. "Pick it up. Pick it up," whispered Hasini. I picked it up, and opened it curiously.

"Meet me at the beach after dinner is over."

Looking over my shoulder was Benny, and as I took a glance at him he grunts. "You've got to be kidding me." I guess he was just surprised that it was me that was getting the chance to speak with the pretty lady for a change.

As dinner concluded I saw Hasini making her way towards the beach. Likewise I followed in her direction. With the moonlight shining full, the water resting easy I saw her in the distance with her hair let down as the wind blew gently through. She seemed all the more beautiful with every moment that passed by, and I am incapable of knowing why. This moment felt so filmy at the back of my mind, but it wasn't like I was in love. Though I did know that cupid wasn't going to warn me before shooting a damn arrow. Walking towards her felt a lot more difficult than I expected. This time around I didn't have the alcohol steaming bravery from within. Hasini kept her eyes steady in sight of the silent sea. I walked next to her and accompanied her, and we both shared a quiet moment; I was the one to break first.

"Is there something you wanted to talk about? Why'd you ask me to meet you here?" I inquired.

She took a fleeting moment and then turned towards me and replied, "I just wanted to apologize for how rudely I behaved earlier today, maybe we can start fresh? As friends?" It didn't take me an ample amount of time to respond, I myself was hoping for a fresh start. Her expression showed how pleased she was to see my reaction. I stood there wondering what to say next, and as I took my sweet time she smiled and paced way back towards the hotel. I had a hard time letting her walk away, with every step she moved further, and I was left hoping to see her smile for a few more hours.

With the courage I was able to build I called out to her, "Are you really going to go back to your hotel room already?"

"Is there something you had in mind," she questioned with a laugh.

Turning to my left I took a look at the sea. "Why don't we learn more about one another," I asked not knowing whether she would even be interested. Her acceptance seemed transparent as she made her way back towards me. With the dark night consuming our surroundings her presence brought the moon to life. The moon always shines bright, but after all these years I actually noticed its magnificence. We spoke for hours; by the end of it she seemed all the more beautiful. At first glance it was her beauty that caught my eyes, her long wavy black hair, the way her mesmerizing hazel eyes almost sealed shut as she laughed her heart away, the way I just wanted to place my hands around her sharp jawline, and her smile, a smile that makes me forget of everything around me.

It was actually who she was that made me feel some type of way. Just after a few hours of conversing I didn't expect to know someone like I understood Hasini. I saw the sadness in joyful eyes when she spoke of her parents. Hasini lost both her parents to a lethal car crash when she was thirteen, leaving her in the care of her uncle. With brief happiness she carried away, telling me of how her uncle treated her like his very own daughter. Though like her parents, he too was taken away from her life while she was away for her first year of university. With all that was drawn from her she remained brave, stuck through and followed her dreams of becoming a journalist. This maybe where she got me. The amount of energy she had while talking about her plans for the future. She carried on about how she wishes to travel around the world and spread notice of stories to help the innocents whom need a hand. How she looks forward to being in love with a man she can consider a friend. Then she went on about how she would like to adopt a child; Sarah came to my eyes.

The time neared 2:00am, and it was probably time for us to head back to the hotel. However, I was waiting till she wanted to leave. At this point even the hours of time I spent with her wasn't enough. She continued going on of the things she has done, or wanted to do for a few more minutes before she felt tired. We then decided to head back to the hotel. As we walked through the courtyard towards the tall glass doors I started to wish that time would sit still, but tonight is the first of many moments I planned to spend with her. Her room was nothing more than a few doors down from mine; saying our goodbyes she leaned in for a hug. Her head pressed against my chest and I knew I wanted this forever, as crazy as it may sound I felt like I was really falling for this girl.

I waved to her as she entered her room, and then opened my own. Closing the door behind me I leaned my back against it. Never have I felt this way, ever! I'm not even too sure if this is love. Today was the first day I have ever crossed paths with her, am I crazy to be calling this love? I saw my face in the mirror next to me, and I was incapable of erasing a harmonious smile off my face. I felt like dancing and jumping around like I just won the lotto.

I laid on my bed with my mind lost in another world. I tried to figure out why I fell for her, and no other before her; the curiosity was killing me. Even with my eyes shut her beauty kept presenting itself. My fingers tapped my chest gently, and I can feel the rise in beats with every moment I thought of her.

I never had the chance, nor will I ever get the opportunity of meeting my birth mother. I will never feel her care, love, and compassion, but Sarah never made me miss it. Sarah was my mother, and I long felt the emptiness of her presence, that is until this very moment. It struck me of how Hasini made me feel new; she reminds me of my mother. Hasini was a strong independent woman, with a dream, someone who desires to not only look out for herself, but for the lives of others as well. You meet many girls, and some may be friends, but no woman ever measures to the standing of a mother. Though when a woman reminds you of your mother, even to the slightest degree you simply do not let her go. I don't know what Hasini feels about me, she may just consider me a friend or her friends' brother, but from this point onward I know she's not someone I can watch leave my life.

~

Around 5:23am I was awaken rudely to a knocking on the door, it was Thiru and Mahat. The two of them were prepared for the wedding, and here I was in my boxers. Apparently they decided to wake me up knowing that I probably came back to my room really late last night. Great call on their part; I might have even missed my sisters wedding. They barged in and took my pack of smokes, while walking out the door Thiru reminded me to call them after I was ready. Standing in front of the bathroom mirror I applied shaving cream to my face, and as the blade stroked down my cheek I had a sudden realization. What if Hasini isn't awake yet? I should probably check to make sure that she woke up as well! Rushing out my room I knocked on her door, I forgot that I remained in my boxers with shaving cream applied all over my face. She opened the door wrapped around in a towel alone, her hair wet, as drips of water kissed her skin.

She began to laugh uncontrollably; I stood still, thinking that I should probably leave; she was wrapped in a towel! I may have really good self-control, but at the end of the day I am still a guy; the thoughts will begin to flow. In the midst of laughing she asked, "You really like stripping in the hallway, don't you?" That's when I realized that I continued to stand there in my boxers, with shaving cream on my face; how embarrassing, especially in front of the girl you want to impress. I watched as she laughed; putting my shame aside, I couldn't resist but to laugh with her. While I was walking away with a smile on my face she called my name.

"Come knock on my door when you go down, this time try to wear more clothes," she joked.

She was one with a good sense of humor, something else I loved about her. I finished shaving and hopped into the shower, to soon be slipping into my clothes. I wore black pants, and I tucked my white shirt and began knotting the black tie around my neck. After throwing on a black blazer, I was out the door walking towards Hasini's room. She too was coming out of her room, I was blown away at how fast she got ready; this girl just gets better and better. In her white saree, she looked breathtaking.

"Hasini, you look gorgeous!" I said; her beauty was really making me nervous.

"Well Arrun, you clean up very nice! Though the boxer look is better on you," she responded.

We shared a brief laugh and made our way down to the lobby where I saw Mahat and Thiru having a smoke over some coffee. Benny was in the opposite direction flirting with the smoking hot receptionist.

"You could at least try not to stare," said Hasini with a smile on her face.

I really need to clean up my act; if I want to impress her I should really stop getting caught in the midst of my stupid activities.

"I'll get us some coffee, we both probably need it after getting two hours of sleep," I suggested.

Some how I managed to escape the embarrassment, after grabbing a cup of coffee I decided to introduce Hasini to Mahat and Thiru first considering the fact that Benny is completely occupied. They were still smoking away, and while walking towards them I had the urge to ask for a smoke as well, but I wasn't sure if Hasini cared or not.

"Guys this is Hasini, she's Rohini's best friend; you guys remember seeing her at dinner right?"

Hasini just remained there in her stance, with a smile on her face; shaking their hands Mahat asked, "Why are you hanging out with Arrun of all people, he's boring." "There's a lot more to him than you think," Hasini praised; I felt great. Who wouldn't feel great seeing the girl they treasured defending them while they are made a mockery of. A few moments after my brothers stopped insulting me, Hasini asked Thiru for a smoke.

"You smoke?" I asked, completely astonished.

"Rarely, I do at times though, just when I have the feel for it. Don't you?" Asked Hasini.

"No, I do; just thought you may feel disgusted by it," I responded.

Laughing hysterically she said, "Don't pretend like you don't smoke just because someone else would care, do as you wish." I swear this girl ceases to amaze me, she keeps saying things to make me tumble deeper in love; if she doesn't fall in love with me by the end of it all I swear I don't know how I'd deal with this heartbreak. I wasn't the only one who was surprised; Mahat and Thiru were pretty speechless themselves.

"You're pretty awesome," screamed Thiru.

"I know right!" She cheered with her tasteful voice.

Mahat standing to my right, came close and whispered, "She's a keeper bro." It seems as if I wasn't the only one enjoying her company, one member at a time she was stealing the hearts of my family.

Being surrounded by family and friends I didn't notice the time fly, Hasini stood at my side the entire morning. It was 11:00am before we even got a moment to check the time, in a brief moment Akil will tie the auspicious thread around Rohinis neck pronouncing them husband and wife according to our birth culture, followed by the exchanging of rings. Standing there amongst family in the midst of those I love, I had to take a brief moment to think of Sarah. Had Sarah been here this very moment this wedding was conducted exactly the way she would've wanted to see it. Though we are all adopted children Sarah took the initiative in making sure we stay close to our roots. She even made the effort to learn more about our culture just so she can teach us about it in the future; a wonderful mother indeed.

The big moment, as Akil grasped hold of the thread bringing it around Rohinis neck he began tying the first of three knots. Rohini held both her hands palm to palm and I saw a tear drop down her cheek, as her eyes came towards me I tried my best to not shed a tear myself, she looked beautiful. With a hand on Rohini's shoulder, Hasini too was looking towards me. While she was looking at me with her smile I had a wild thought of one day having the chance to marry Hasini, keeping her for myself. With the third knot the confetti began to fly, my three brothers jumped in joy, while Asha hugged Rohini tight. Emotions were flying everywhere, I felt Hasini wrapping her arm around me, leaning her head against my shoulder. Smiling with a glance at Hasini I turned to have a look at everyone in celebration; this moment was irreplaceable.

Celebration continued through the day and by nightfall it was time to party. We sat around the bar as a family, the same bar where I met Hasini for the first time. Ironically both Hasini and I were sitting in the same spot we were before. I'm just hoping that this time around she doesn't tear me apart with her "kind" words. The drinks flowed over laughs, along with cheesy speeches from all the members of the family. The best time of the night came when we hit the dance floor, I may not be so great talking to the ladies, but I can sure as hell impress them on the dance floor. We danced to our hearts content; with ten minutes remaining the DJ began playing music for the couples. For most of us it was our queue to take a seat; Rohini and Akil sharing a moment of their first dance, Asha with her boyfriend, Benny with some random girl he sweet-talked, and Mahat and Thiru were far too busy at the bar once again.

I took a seat next to Hasini at one of the empty tables on the side of the dance floor. "Aren't you going to ask me to dance," she questioned. I can't believe I didn't even think of asking her! For a moment I gazed at the dance floor, and then held grasp of her hand. With a gap between the newly wed and us I put my hands on her waist as she wrapped her arms around my neck. With the night sky glowing of bright stars, the dance floor was becoming packed with couples in every direction. Though my full attention was on Hasini alone. In that moment I felt the presence of no one around us, it was only she and I accompanied by the stars and the moon. "Brittle Pieces," by Zemmy was playing in the back; with the music creating the right atmosphere I saw it for the first time. Her eyes glowed of something different, something I haven't seen in all others. I had the urge of thinking that she felt the same way as I did, but I can't find the courage to ask till I knew for sure. Ten minutes in length, I felt like I was dancing with her for an eternity.

The DJ played the concluding song of the party. Everyone ran back on to the floor jumping and screaming, but Hasini and I remained grasped to one another with no reaction to everyone going crazy around us. Asha and Rohini were the ones to first bump into us. Bringing us back to reality, and with a glance at one another she drifted away with the girls. On the middle of the dance floor I stood, with both my hands against the back of my head feeling more alive than ever. I watched as Hasini would constantly turn back and take glances back at me; it was just an amazing feeling. My brothers including Akil soon circled me; I tagged along with them, and danced like a bunch of crazy people.

When the party commenced it was about 3:15am, and you could see the tiredness among all. Countless people started making their way back to their respective hotel rooms. I stood there for a moment with Benny,

Mahat, and Thiru having a smoke. Among the crowd of friends stepped forward Hasini; coming toward us she asked me, "Heading back upstairs soon?"

"You three don't mind if I head back with Hasini right?" I asked, hoping my brothers won't be upset.

"No you go ahead, we're probably going to go sleep too," replied Thiru

Making our way back to our rooms we remained moderately quiet; neither one of us broke the silence till we made our way to the elevator.

"Great wedding, right?" I asked unable to bare the peace.

"It was amazing," responded Hasini with enthusiasm.

"I'm actually pretty drunk, I don't even remember drinking that much though," she shouted.

Looking at her with a smile I responded, "Oh trust me, we all drank plenty enough today." Continuously blabbing away she thought she might have trouble finding her room, so I accompanied her all the way to the door. Once she walked in, I turned towards the direction of mine.

"Going back to your room already?" She asked.

Turning back towards her I asked, "Why, is there something you had in mind?" We laughed for a brief moment reversing the roles from the night before. She stepped into the bathroom to change; I took my blazer off and loosened my tie before getting comfortable on a couch next to her bed. When she came out she took seat on the bed, and we continued talking of the moments through the day; even our dance. An hour in I thought I should maybe hint how I feel, just to see her reaction, and so I did.

"Its funny how we just met yesterday, or the night before; though I don't remember the incident much. But I feel like I've known you my entire life, and that probably never happens for many people. The sight of you standing under the moonlight remains in my eyes, and now I have the imprint of your beauty when we shared a dance. I've met a lot of girls, many of whom I've even tried dating, but none of them were able to make me feel anything special. You did, and I don't know how you pulled the string but I am in no way able to let you go. I was never able to see my birth mother, and then a year ago I had to lose the mother who never let me feel at loss. After you came along all that heartache I had locked up disappeared, leaving life nourishing me from within. You know you could say some."

I didn't realize that I was looking down while pouring my thoughts to her. When I took a glance towards her she was fast asleep. It was such an annoying but amusing moment, I finally gained the courage to express myself and she's asleep; just my luck. Lying on her side, with her back turned towards me she slept, more beautiful than sleeping beauty herself. Turning off the night lamp to our side, I took rest on the couch.

Chapter 3 - About Time

Freshly brewed the smell of coffee made my morning rise calm. "Good morning," Hasini greeted; she was already showered and in the midst of packing for our flights later in the afternoon. It then hit me that we'll all be catching flights in a few hours, and we'll be heading back to our daily routines. It was a blessing to not wake up with a hangover, considering the amount of partying we did last night. While she topped off her packing I quickly made way into my room and threw everything into a suitcase; after all I was going to go home and throw everything around my room anyway.

I was in such a rush, all just to spend time with Hasini. After showering and getting ready for the day I sat on my bed taking down the remaining sips of the coffee Hasini brought me. Waiting for her knock at the door I sat wishing she heard the things I had to say last night. It was just my luck that she had to fall asleep while I vented my feelings, but its not like I won't get another chance. I have to tell her again, if I don't I may risk losing her; that wasn't an option.

"Don't you lock your room? You're going to get raped!" Shouted Hasini.

"You've got jokes," I replied in my sarcastic tone. Dragging her out the door with me, we made way to the buffet; I was starving. The rest of the guys were already seated at a table. There wasn't any room for us at the table, so Hasini and I took a seat at another table for two. We had a pleasing conversation; she even proposed we hangout sometime when we're back in Toronto. I felt elated with the exchange we had over the breakfast buffet, though my mind would partially regret every passing moment where she didn't know how I felt.

Time turned quickly, and a weekend of memories was about to end. Waiting for cabs to the airport we took seat in the hotel lobby. Rohini and Akil were about to head off on their honeymoon; the rest of us will be back to our boring jobs and regular routines. It took about thirty minutes, but the first cab showed up with room for four people. With others willing to wait Rohini, Akil, Hasini, and I were the first on our way to the airport. The drive to the airport consisted talks of the memories we made this past weekend; upon arriving I was first to be out unloading luggage from the trunk. Hasini remained alongside myself while Rohini and Akil made way to get their boarding pass.

"Last night, in the hotel room; I heard everything you said," she said.

My eyes pound open with an unstoppable beat within my heart; it was disbelief. She calmly grabbed her luggage and rolled it away with a smile, while I was left feeling remote from my body. Clicking back in I grabbed my bags and ran behind her.

"Hasini, STOP!" I shouted.

"You heard everything? So you weren't asleep?" I asked, extremely curious.

She stood with a continual grin on her face; it was pure torture. I needed to know; looking down at her passport and ticket she once again calmly drifted her head side to side. Stepping closer to her, standing eye for an eye I asked, "Hasini, What are you thinking? I need to know what you're thinking."

"That day when you tried talking to me at the bar for the first time, I was pissed at you. In those moments, I really did not feel like seeing your face. After realizing you were Rohini's brother, I found myself laughing in my room, all alone. It's been quite a while since I laughed like that. From that moment till the instance you saw me standing by shore your face kept popping in my head. Then later that night when I was walking back towards the hotel, I hoped for you to call me back, and you did. I find it very difficult to tell people about the struggles I've faced, but in your presence it came without my notice. I put my trust in you faster than I can do with any other. Though our dance is when I knew I completely fell for you. Even when lying in my bed I pretended to sleep in hopes you'd say something, and once again you made my hopes come true. I don't want this trip to be the end of our journey."

Grasping Hasini close with no distance to spare I saw it in her eyes once again. This time around I wasn't going to let my chance go; I kissed her, something I wanted to do this entire weekend. Letting breath go slowly she remained embraced to me; for the first time I felt love.

"Aren't I just like cupid?" Interrupted a voice.

It was Rohini, it seems as if this were her intention the whole time. If I didn't love my sister enough before, I sure as hell am thankful for her being now. If it weren't for Rohini, Hasini and I would have probably been two people who never got off to a great start. By the time all four of us got our boarding passes the others arrived from the hotel. Their reactions after seeing Hasini and myself together were quite priceless; Thiru, Mahat, and Asha were glad I was finally able to find someone who taught me to love. Then there was Benny; he had a real hard time trying to figure out how she liked me.

"You? She likes you? Man, this is unbelievable; no offence bro but how can anyone fall in love with someone like you? You got no game!"

What an annoying creature he was, but it was amusing in its own way. If I were to actually analyze it even I'd be curious. Hasini did though, and to me that's more than enough. My flight back to Toronto won't be an easy one; Hasini being a journalist is taking flight to India to cover a story, and she won't be back for a few weeks. Knowing that she's mine is relieving enough to help me pass through the next few weeks. Hasini's flight happened to be before the rest of ours; saying goodbye wasn't easy but it wasn't forever.

~

Those weeks weren't easy, but being able to talk through video call accompanied by my time spent at work the weeks flew. When she was back we began what I hoped to be a lifetime of memories.

Before we knew it, a year passed with the same love between us. A year together and yes, we did have our fights; some were nasty but we were always able to get through it. Our relationship worked so well because we were never ones to act like high school kids in love. In majority our time spent together was better defined as friends in love. In fact since that weekend in the Dominican we haven't really expressed our love in words.

The day October 12th 2012, I invited Hasini to a spot she once took me a few months back. It was a place where Hasini's father took her as a child to watch stars and the moon. After the passing of her father her uncle also took her there at times when she'd cry trying to forget. She loved that place; it's where she'd go to find peace in mind. It was around 10:00pm and when we arrived the water was already glistening with moonlight amidst the significant amount of stars. Standing near the edge of the cliff the atmosphere was just right. I dropped on one knee, as she stood stunned.

"We've only been together for a year, but a year in the world you take me to feels like a lifetime and a lifetime is exactly what I want to spend with you. I'll never be great at expressing my feelings and you know that. But here, at this place where the most important men of your life have protected you I ask, can I be lucky enough to join their company? Hasini, I love you. Will you marry me?"

"Yes, Yes, Yes! Holy shit! Of course I will! " Screamed Hasini.

After placing the ring on her finger she tackled me with tears of thrill running down her cheeks. With a breath of fresh air I felt relieved; I may have cheated a bit though. A few months back Rohini told me about a conversation she had with Hasini. One about the possibility of marriage in our future, with hints roaming in the air I felt all my thoughts toward tonight's decision were well worth it.

Everyone back at the house already knew that I was going to propose to Hasini so it didn't come as a surprise when we walked into the house together. Similar to the day Rohini and Akil made their big announcement; we once again popped champagne in celebration. Times were great, and the bond of family was irreplaceable. Standing amongst family, I found myself wishing for all the hard times to be over.

Chapter 4 - Good Things Come and Go

Four months since the announcement Hasini and Arrun decided to put off the wedding plans for a year or so. Hasini had a huge story to cover, one that needed the attention of a global audience; she needed the space and time. A few months back after the trip to the Dominican, Hasini left for India. What she found there was a story for the ages. Being a journalist you can only dream of some day getting hold of such. When she came back from India, she became somewhat obsessed with exposing the story. She never told anyone about the story, minus her co-workers; some wouldn't care, others couldn't be trusted.

While in India she stumbled upon a story, one of Marona Duranjis son, Miran. Miran is the youngest of Maronas two sons, the other being Verone. Verone was quiet and much more reserved when it came to violence, nothing like his father. Then there was Miran, completely reckless and Maronas favored son. Miran is second in head after his father when it comes to leading the criminal activity. He was responsible for many of the murders, child trafficking, and drug circulations around the world. Yet his actions are not known to most, but why would they be? Ninety-five percent of the world's population did not even care for the stranger next to them. Hasini was different; she was part of the special five percent that dreamt of making a difference in the world. Journalism was her tool to make things right, and once grasping hold of this story she turned all attention towards it.

A lot of important people turned their head the other way when it came to criminal activity orchestrated by the Duranji's, but Hasini is one for the people, and she kept tabs on all events led by the family. According to the word she received, Miran was in Toronto. Kidnapped women were to get transported from Canada back to India to be sold to the wealthy. Violence against women has become a major concern in India as of late, and the leading cause of it is because of men like Miran. The location of the warehouse was quite sketchy, but it was her only chance to get the job done. Catching some footage or quality pictures will put an immense hole in the Duranji Empire.

Driving up to the warehouse her safest way to capture photos would be through the consuming forest. With the time of the sky in her hands it would be easier for her to capture everything unnoticed in the dark. Among the trees and bushes it would be greatly difficult for one of the henchmen to notice being documented, or so she thought. Hasini was not alone on this, she brought along her partner Trent. However what she did not know is that Trent was not one to trust. Miran is not someone who would have loose ends lying around, and buying Trent's loyalty did not come at any difficulty.

One flash, one flash from the camera is all that it took for one of Miran's henchmen to come of Hasini's location. "Pack everything quick, we have to get out of here," shouted Hasini. Trent standing motionless with his head down could not find his words. Pulling Trent by the arm Hasini did not want to leave without him, she knew getting caught would not end well for them.

"Trent we have to leave! Now! Please come!" She screamed.

"Hasini, I'm sorry," replied Trent, holding his head low in shame.

Something was wrong and Hasini knew it; there is no longer use in fleeing. Fate was no longer in her hands, and with a deep exhale she closed her eyes. The aggression was clear, but she was too consumed in fear to have a glance of her surroundings. No future is ever clear, but they do come with plans; the thing about plans is that they can be altered in an instant. Pushed to her knees, she heard the cries for freedom from the women held captive at the warehouse. With fear and sorrow striking war in her mind the tears found its way out.

"Open your eyes," demanded Miran.

Miran's sinful being was well dissolved in his voice. Hasini opened her eyes and was received by Miran standing at six feet in height; bald with a heavy beard, and a gruesome scar above his right eye his presence equivalent to that of a monster. Behind him were about twelve henchmen who were equally provoking fear in all. Bending down looking Hasini directly in they eye he began to speak.

"Tell me, what exactly was your plan? Did you actually think you could just walk in here, to my place and expose my activities to the world? Do *you really think of yourself as a hero? You know, occasionally some men come along and try to be the savior, and guess what it never works out for them. You're the first woman to have actually even tried to bring down the Empire and for that I applaud you. Bravo! Hey, you know what? Take a look to your left; you see all those women standing there chained and beaten, were they the ones you tried to save? I want you to listen carefully; their fate is sealed, they are going to be passed around from man to man, generating me money and you can't do a thing about it! You know what you're quite the beauty yourself, maybe you'd like to join them?"*

"Please, I beg you. Let us go and I promise not to speak a word," cried Hasini.

Laughing hysterically, Miran took out his gun; walking towards some of the women chained to the side he grinned taking shots ruthlessly. While turning back towards Hasini he screamed, "Do I look like an idiot to you? Do I?" Grabbing Hasini by the hair he hauled her to the mirror leaning against the metal beam and smashed her head into it till the blood initiated flow. The blood ran but she remained awake to the horror as she tried getting up.

"Grab her," shouted Miran, looking toward his henchmen's. With two animals lifting her by the arm Hasini was beginning to loss consciousness, and as the blood dropped her fate may have been sealed. Miran laughing psychotically sat on top of a table next to the now shattered mirror, wishing to see Hasini drowned, "Dump her," he commanded. Dragging her hopeless soul, Miran's henchmen began to dip her head into a glass tank of water.

Hasini knew in her mind, times were coming to an end. She pleaded for her life, but there is no pleading that was going to save her from the insanity that is Miran. When faced with death we can do three things, hope you will live to see another day, worry about what comes after death, or you can simply embrace it. Hasini did not fight back the force of the henchmen; she calmly closed her eyes and thought about Arrun one last time. She knew her time was over, but in those moments she could not help but think of the life she could have had with him. Hasini could not help but think of how he will take it; will he move on? Can he take another loss? Memories came to her, and as she began to struggle for breath, she departed with a smile, with thoughts of Arrun gracing her mind.

Stepping down from the table Miran spoke in secrecy to one of his trusted henchman, "Put her in the car and make it look like an accident; push the car off a bridge or something, no traces! As for the other three bodies, just bury them. Don't forget to make sure Trent has an alibi, and get the rest of this girls story from him."

Breaking from his follower he turned towards the crowd of women, now trembling in horror; with one glance he let them know what happens when people come in his way.

After making sure transport for the women was set, Miran took leave of the warehouse. Shortly after, Miran's henchmen began commencing on his orders; Hasini now a soulless corpse was being carried to the near distance where her car was parked in secrecy. Then henchmen were extremely careful in making sure her death looked like an unfortunate accident.

A couple miles from the warehouse there was a bridge, one that is never really busy. With the time being around 3am, it was the ideal time to end Hasini's chapter. The time 3:23am, breaking through the concrete barrier Hasini's car is now gradually making way towards the body of water. As history has proved, many who want to contribute to the world must face death early. At times the world loses a savior, but ones death at times has a bigger impact on another individual, over what they could have done for the world. It is a tragedy that true love had to die young; Hasini's loss will surely have an impact on Arrun.

Chapter 5 - A Tragic Beginning

It has been such a long day; Hasini was busy with something so I decided to finish prepping for her surprise. After proposing to Hasini a few months back I thought it would be reasonable for us to live together. I was already earning more than I needed with my current job, and with the amount of money Sarah left for each one of us I was able to purchase a beautiful lakeshore condo in Toronto.

Early in the afternoon I got hold of the key and the new place was beautiful, really modern looking. I liked the open flow of the condo, but what really sold me was the view. It was remarkably beautiful during the day, and I could only imagine what I was in store for at night, with the lights of the city shining bright. Initially I thought moving in was going to be a hassle, but with the help of the movers the job was a lot easier than expected. By the time midnight struck I was already settled in; the new appliances were in, furniture in place, and me oh my, my brand new TV had me confused if I could love Hasini the same.

It was pretty late in the night when I stepped on to the balcony with my cup of coffee. Placing a cigarette between my lips, I had seen the best of both worlds. My condo was placed in an angle; so when I look to my left I have a beautiful view of the calm lake, resting easy with its roots, and no destruction by men. Towards the right was the view of buildings towering over one another; it's weird that mankind usually destroys the planet, yet they can make a city of lights seem just as stunning.

Though the city lights were marvelous, I stuck to what the Earth had to offer. The time 3:23am, glancing over the admirable water, with the combination of coffee and a cigarette, I was left thinking of the new journey I will embark on with my beautiful fiancée.

Hasini was not going to know about my surprise for her till the morning, and seeing how she probably would not even call this late into the night I should probably sleep.

~

I was only asleep for a few hours before I started receiving an abundant of calls. They were from an unfamiliar number, so I ignored it. It continued. Though after some time I was not able to deal with the annoyance, nor was I able to sleep. However when I answered the call I was immediately placed to shock, it was from a Staff Sargent John Collins.

"Hey Arrun, this is Staff Sargent John Collins calling. I hate to be the one to break it to you but there has been an accident. We were able to

retrieve a phone from the scene, with a number last dialed to you. Do you know a Hasini Ravichandra?"

"Yes! Officer she's my fiancée! Is she okay? Where is she?" I inquired, already thinking the worst.

"Arrun, I need you to remain quiet for a brief moment and hear what I have to say. Sometime last night, possibly early in the morning Hasini's car crashed into the barrier of a bridge, eventually submerging under water. Hasini seemed to have sustained serious trauma to the head, and suffocation from being trapped under water. My apologies Arrun, but we were too late. By the time we came to know of the incident, Hasini had already passed. We currently transported her body to St.Micheals Hospital and would like for you to come there, so we can speak in further detail."

"Arrun! Arrun? Are you there?" called out the officer.

No, it isn't possible. It has to be a sick, cruel joke right? My body felt numb, my phone surged to the ground, and I dropped to my knees. It was hard trying to gain breath, I did not want believe it. I didn't believe it; I rushed to St.Micheals Hospital, the whole time praying for that phone call to be a prank. Walking through the emergency doors, a cold chill devoured my body. I never felt this fear before, I wondered if anything can scare me more.

I never liked the environment of hospitals, a place of life and death; a hospital is the perfect explanation of what lays between heaven and hell. There were strangers everywhere, some mourning a loss, some in queue for death and life, and some celebrating new arrivals. Then there was me, torn in confusion; hoping for something that probably just won't go my why. Receiving a light tap on my shoulder, I turned to an officer.

> "Officer, don't say it. Please, I beg you! What the fuck are you doing! This isn't funny; this is a sick-fucking joke isn't it! Officer, I can't take it, please just tell me it's a lie. Please! Of course it's a lie, I mean I was going to surprise her today. I bought a beautiful condo, we were going to marry and start a beautiful life together. She can't be gone, she just can't. You're lying! Tell me she's there behind those doors, with her beautiful smile; she's testing to see how much I love her, right? She's everything to me, if she's gone…"

"Arrun! Get yourself together! I need you to walk with me, it is going to be hard, but you have to deal with it. She is gone!" Shouted the officer, as I stared upon him; still hoping for everything to work in my favor.

With ever step we drew closer to the truth, my denial was beginning to fade. I knew what lies ahead will not be easy to handle, but I needed to know. Surging past the officer, unable to hold the negative anticipation I forced through the doors. With corpses lying lonesome, Sargent John Collins grasped me. He pulled me back and walked me towards a figure covered under a white cloth.

My hands nervously shivered, making pace towards the cloth I did not want the truth. Pulling it over, thousands of emotions filled my thoughts, but I was not able to speak. A tear dropped, and emotions began to pour.

"No, No, No, Hasini...No! Hasini, talk to me! Please! Hasini, smile Hasini, I don't want to see you like this. I need you Hasini, Hasini! We were meant to grow old together; you can't leave me before we begin our lives. We were going to have children, a son as amusing as me, and a daughter as beautiful and loving as you. How am I to keep going now, without you? Hasini, please!"

"Arrun, we need to go now," said officer John Collins.

I wasn't able to bear it; I rushed back out the door. I was angry, emotions took over, and I was punching walls, smashing everything in sight. The officer was the one to bring me down; he took me to the floor and shouted, "Arrun! You need to calm down!" Hasini was gone, but I was the one who felt soulless. Life no longer had a purpose, and things were never going to be the same.

Chapter 6 - Life Had Other Plans

Three months passed since Hasini left my life, and things never found their way back into place. I constantly visited the bridge where the accident took place, staring endlessly over the body of water that took her away from me. Today was no different; I stood over with a flask of whisky trying to forget. Forgetting was never a reasonable option, how do you forget love that was real. At most, all I was able to do is try and keep my mind off it, even if it were temporary.

It was hard; it was hard to believe how things flipped upside down so quickly. You never get warnings before accidents, and I knew it, but I just could not accept it. With every ticking second I remember looking into her eyes and feeling whole; her parting completely broke me.

At first I was ready to walk alone

Keeping the anticipation of a long journey in thought

Cross Roads: Pick a Path

A journey I was confident of boarding alone

Without my desire

She came

Standing shoulder to shoulder at the entrance of darkness

With every moment that passed on our journey we grew closer

The darkness became brighter

I was able to see life in a different light

The missing piece

Right there

The middle of it all

She left

Making the light a darkness

Once again

Leaving me to question it all

Why? Why come, to go

Standing unable to move back or forward

Lost in the woods I must remain

Until I forget

But will I ever?

Days passed; I often found myself sitting on the floor of my condo, leaning against the wall with alcohol as my only companion. My family has often tried to get me back to being the Arrun they love, but the Arrun the world once knew died the day Hasini stopped breathing. I wasn't even able to close my eyes without her presence aching my soul, and as much as it hurt, it helped.

It didn't take me too long to close the entire world out; at first alcohol was the companion. Soon the presence of a dark room made things easier. The slash in my mind became worse, and forgetting never seemed so difficult. At times I could not even bare it; I needed more help. My family was always there for me in times where I needed to talk, but I simply did not want to associate with the rest of the world. Drugs; never thought I would even have the thought of turning to them again some day, but it did seem like a reasonable escape. I have smoked marijuana back in high school, and university, but back in those days it was more of a stress-reliever. Now I just want it so I can forget, and maybe remember the good.

In the rare occasions I stepped out of the condo, I observed a man who clearly had his hands on marijuana. I once overheard someone call him Remone, after a few days of observing his actions I decided to walk over and speak to him.

"Hey man, are you selling?" I asked.

"What are you, a fucking fed," asked Remone.

"No, just someone who needs to get his mind off a few things," I replied.

"I've seen you observing me lately, you're creepy as fuck dude. I don't know if I can trust you," replied Remone in a hesitant tone.

"So you do have, come on man; I really need it. Shit just hasn't been easy for me. I've got money bro, I promise. You're the first person I've even spoken to in a while." I pleaded.

"You just get creepier by the second don't you. So you've got a problem eh? Why don't you explain that a bit?" He asked.

"My fiancée died in a car accident three months back! I can't get my fucking mind off her! I didn't come here to be your fucking friend, are you going to sell to me, or what? Cause I'm sure I can find someone to take my money," I shouted.

"Chill bro, chill! Damn, I didn't see that coming. All right man, you do seem to be having it rough, here's three deagles, on me. Next time I won't be showing you pity, I will need the money," replied Remone, while he slowly handed me some marijuana.

Walking away from Remone, I decided to make a quick stop at the local liquor store. Whisky is what I often drank; it was always strong enough to get me drunk. When I made way to the cashier she took a look at me, she was a fairly elderly women. "You could use a trim and shave son, you'd get all the ladies going crazy," she commented, with smile. She was kind, and she reminded me of Sarah so I was able to front a fake smile. I noticed my change when I wasn't even able to say a simple thank you, I am far from the person I once was.

It didn't take me that long to roll up the marijuana as soon as I made it back to my condo on the twenty-sixth floor. With first draw, the smoke swished its way down to my lungs. Captivating me from inside, my mind tangled into a million thoughts; and as I took continuous draws, the thoughts began to process. Clouds of smoke filled the room, and leaning back on my couch it was kind of beautiful watching the clouds drift as the sea.

The joint didn't last too long, and I did not hesitate to immediately crack open the bottle of whisky. The resplendent sea of clouds continued to drift throughout, and leaning down I closed my eyes. It became easier; with the company of substance I was able to remember the moments. The anger of Hasini's face when we first met, the way she talked endlessly of her life and dreams witnessed by the glazing moon, and of course the moment I knew for sure. We were eye to eye on the dance floor, with no distance between us, and none but the moon to watch over us. I realized something then, the moon nurtured the love between Hasini and myself; it was under the presence of the moon and the stars where some of the most memorable moments were made.

A few gulps of alcohol, the calm feeling of memories helped me feel alive, but it didn't last too long as I was interrupted by a rude knocking on my door.

Chapter 7 - Change Is Good?

They did not give up; it was the entire family who stood before me. They have tried to come over a numerous amount of times, in attempts to talk to me. It always failed, not like today would make a difference. Benny was the first to rush in.

"What the hell is this," he questioned, with an expression of disbelief.

"You're smoking Marijuana? Who the hell do you think you are, a dumb teenager? How much longer are you going to be like this Arrun, you look like shit! You've lost your job because you stopped going, you live in a nice place that you've turned in a hellhole. Like really? Get some fucking light in this place! What's with all this drinking? If you want to drink, you've got three brothers who'd love to go out with you sometime. Let us in bro, we need you to be the Arrun we love. We don't even know you anymore."

"What do you know," I grumbled.

Everyone drifted to a state of shock; it has been a really long time since they have actually heard me speak. I have kept loads of emotions locked in for the past few months, and it must be the alcohol, but I could not bare people speaking without knowing my pain.

"What do you know? No! Tell me what the hell do you know? Do you know what it feels like to lose someone you love? When we lost Sarah it was easier, we were able to deal with it together, why? Well its because we all loved her the same, but it wasn't like that with Hasini. No words can express how much I loved her. Every time I close my eyes, she's right there! What am I supposed to do? You want me to talk to you guys about her? Do you really think that'll help me forget her? Cause it won't! Right here, this spot right here is where I dropped to my knees when the officer called me. She's gone Benny, she's gone, and there's nothing I can do that will bring her back to me! Rohini, how would it feel if you lost Akil? Do you think you'd be able to handle it? I feel like dying Rohini! I just want to die! I can't bear to live in a world without her. I want to just let my life go, but is it what Hasini would want? What if I die and that's it? I can't let those memories die along with me just to escape a world without her. Asha, remember the amount of times you've told me how lucky I was? Thiru, Mahat, do you guys remember her with us in the lobby of the hotel that one time? How she smiled? That day in the mortuary, when I removed the white clothe and saw her lay there without life. I knew that I'll never see that smile again...it crushed me; I died in those very seconds."

Dropping to my knees, I could not bear it anymore. The locked emotions, turned tears; banging the floor, I fell to my back. Thiru and Mahat picked me up, placing me back on the couch; they sat next to me trying to console a shattered soul. My tears continuously dropped, and as I took a look up, Benny stood without words. Asha and Rohini both in tears themselves; my family has never seen me cry before and I did not want this to happen. But there is only so much a person could hold back before they break, and I could not bear it anymore.

Benny leaning down towards me began to speak, "I'm sorry, I didn't know you were holding back so much. Arrun, we need you to let us back in though." I wanted them to be back, but at the same time, being alone seemed more therapeutic.

They remained for an hour more before they left; no one spoke. We all just sort of sat in a circle; it must have been hard for them to say anything. Neither one of them had a clue about the heartache I was holding back.

Soon after they left I once again resorted to intoxication as my escape, it was the only thing that helped.

With everyday that passed, my methods for escape got worse. I began seeing Remone often. Never really spoke to him, just got what I needed and made way in my own direction. Time was not healing these wounds, six months passed since Hasini's passing, and life was still just as dreadful. Getting involved in something may help, but for now the inebriation eases me enough.

I knew that I was personally allowing my life to fall apart. I'm practically broke, and without the alcohol and marijuana I became unable to function.

~

The time was 2:34am, and not content to my daily dose I decided to meet up with Remone who lives approximately two blocks away. When I gave him a call, he asked me to meet me in the alleyway behind his condo. It was an abnormally quiet night in the streets of downtown Toronto. I was making a turn around the corner when I saw a few cars surrounded by a cluster of men. These guys did not look like any ordinary citizens; there was something wrong about them. I continued making way towards the alleyway when I was stopped by one of the men. "Who are you here to see," he questioned. "Remone," I responded; the man did not speak another word, he simply moved over to the side and let me pass.

There had to be a reason for all this hostility, but it didn't really bug me. I just wanted to get the marijuana and leave. I was left in awe when I walked deeper into the alleyway; Marona Duranji, one of the world's most dreaded men stood in my presence. He has been in the news a numerous amount of times; many want him dead, but that is difficult with the support of the government officials he has got on a global scale. Nevertheless, even the criminal phenomenon couldn't get my mind off things.

Marona was too far into discussion with a few other individuals to acknowledge my presence; but Remone did recognize my arrival. "Arrun," he called out with enthusiasm. It didn't make sense to me, because we weren't even that close. With every step he took forward he harassed me about the money I have been expected to pay up. For the past few weeks I have been telling Remone that I will pay him the next day, but it was just my method of trying to push back as far as I can.

"Hey Buddy, you've got that money you owe me?" He asked.

"Remone, I don't have it today man, but I'll have it for sure tomorrow!" I replied.

> "Oh right, that's totally fine with me. I'm guessing you'd like for me to pass you another gram of marijuana? So you can head back home and smoke till you stop crying of your dead fiancée."

The way Remone spoke, it pulled chords. He was triggering a rage from within, a form of temper I have never felt before. I could have let the anger get the best of me, but anger is yet to save lives. Besides, it is obvious that he's linked to the really friendly looking people around me; hitting him may end up being the death of me. Death was not the issue though; it was more about waiting to see how far he goes.

Looking around I noticed that he was making me look like a joke, some of the men around us were laughing, and it was pretty obvious that I am now the center of attention. There is only so much I can bare allowing him to speak. Looking to my left I noticed that I even caught the attention of Marona. But there was a flaw in reality in that very moment, a few meters from Marona a man pulled out his pistol, setting aim for the kingpin himself.

I don't think my thought process has ever worked so quickly, I had two options. I could either watch as Marona gets shot, and then watch to see if the shooter gets away, or I can try and stop the shooter. Was risking my life to save some criminal really worth it though? For the greater good it would be better to just let him die, but maybe I can use this as an opportunity. An opportunity is exactly how I saw it; rushing towards Marona I saw his eyes opening wide in shock. Running just past him I tackled the shooter to the ground.

With the shooter on the ground, I received a bullet through my right shoulder. I can't remember the last time I saw my own blood, but the wound with the river of blood flowing was definitely mine. Lying there on my back, I gazed deep into the sky, and wondered if this could be the end? That's when I realized that I should not fear death, and I should not allow death to get me so easily. The only way to keep the memories Hasini and I shared, is if I remain alive.

As my eyes began to close, I prayed to wake up to life once again. I wanted to wake up to a new life, one where death and loss would no longer be able to continuously torture me.

Part 2: There's Good In Bad

Chapter 8 - A Welcomed Challenge

It was so easy; I thought the mental torture of killing someone would drive me insane, but it felt great. It felt great to be the one to take. I have become so accustomed to losing lives around me, that even something as terrifying as murder made me feel better.

I watched as the dead body was dragged away by two henchmen. Remone was ecstatic; he came and embraced me like we were family. I would have never thought I would be a criminal, but I have to say, it helped me a lot. My mind became more focused on the man I killed over the loss of Hasini. I started to believe that actions like this can help me build a wall, one to block out her death.

Many of the guys were showering me with praises, and it felt completely odd. I mean, I killed a person, but they promote me as a hero or something. Out in the real world, where the normal people walk, what I did today would not have been accepted in a similar fashion. I was not complaining though; I mean I wasn't speaking much, just listening as the rest of the men spoke, but I felt a sense of belonging.

Remone was the one to offer me a ride home; seeing how I didn't really know any of the other guys, it made sense to go with him. On our way home we drove through the bridge, the bridge where the accident took place. Looking out the window, I stared upon the easy resting water, as I always have. Though this time around, my constant wishes for Hasini seemed to have disappeared.

"You good man?" Asked Remone, curious of my silence.

"Yeah, just trying to figure out the last few hours," I responded, as I continued to look out the window.

I had no intention of venting or whining about Hasini any longer, to anyone. I have an opportunity here, a second chance to try and feel alive again, and continuously crying about the past wont help. As a software engineer I can be a very valuable asset to many companies. I can make the money that a lot of people would wish for, I can continue living in a great condo, drive fancy cars, and most of all, be with my family. I don't want to do it anymore though, I can't. Going back to that routine lifestyle is just going to bring back old scars. Besides, I'm already too deep to get out of the water now.

"Arrun man, you're probably drenched in thoughts right now. I don't blame you either, those last few hours were pretty damn hectic. First off, I owe you an apology. Mentioning your fiancée last night, that wasn't

cool. It's just the way I talk to most of my customers; I don't really care about them, I sell and they give me money, that's it. Earlier today, when you pulled out my holstered gun, I was thinking that I really fucked up! If you were to have shot any of our men, you would have died, and then after you were dealt with, I would have gotten killed for being so stupid. But man oh man! You've got some serious nerve my friend, like where the hell did that even come from? BANG! It's like a scene from a movie; it just keeps playing over and over again in my head. Honestly bro, you really impressed Marona; impressing the king of the empire, that's not easy. You my friend are something different, and we're going to be family now brother, and trust me you have no clue of the life you're in for."

Remone just kept speaking endlessly, and I really wanted him to shut up, but I would momentarily look over and simply grin. What would I even say? I mean, I didn't even know what was going through my head when I wanted to kill the guy, how am I supposed to explain it to anyone else? His apology seemed sincere enough for me; I could tell he was trying to get along, and the least I could do was try and be his friend.

It only took us twenty minutes to get home, but it felt like such a long drive. While I was getting out of the car Remone called out to me, "Don't forget, we leave for India in a week! Get all your shit done." I didn't even consider the amount of work that I had cut out for me. I had to manage selling the condo, even the furniture, and I didn't even know how I was going to let my family know about everything.

~

A week's time drifted by pretty fast, mostly because majority of it went by with me trying to find a buyer for the condo. I thought my condo would sell easily, seeing how it's located in downtown Toronto. I guess I will have to settle with renting it out for now, and it maybe easier, this way I won't have to worry about selling my furniture either. Who knows, maybe I will return to my life here someday; though I don't really plan on doing so.

I can finally bear seeing my face in the mirror again. I managed to actually get out of my place for a trim at the local barber. It actually felt kind of nice to be able to see my face, and not feel like a complete cave man.

Remone should be dropping by in an hour or so. Our flight is scheduled to leave at 11am, and with the time being around 8am right now; it's probably the appropriate time to write the letter to my family.

To my caring family,

I know I've really pushed you guys out the past few months. It's because I can't be that same Arrun that you all used to love. Its like I lost all care in the world; I'm not able to love like I once did, I can't sit around and laugh, and I want you guys all to remember me for the Arrun I once was. Rohini, you're probably the first to read this. I wanted you to read it first because it'd be better if you explain this to the family. I'm going to be leaving to India; in fact by the time you read this, I'll probably be gone. I don't know when or if I'll come back; I need this though, I need it to feel alive again. What I'm going to be doing there, I can't share. Rohini, I'd really appreciate it if none of you guys come looking for me. I need the time and space.

Love,

Arrun.

While sitting down on the couch I was curious, of what cross roads my life will meet. To this point everything has just been unforeseen, and for some odd reason I do not think it is going to change any time soon. Feeling a consistent vibration in my pocket I noticed Remone was calling. It was almost 10am, and after letting Remone know I was on my way down I sent Rohini a quick text. "Could you swing by my place today," it read, but I was hesitating to press send. I could not stop questioning whether I was doing the right thing or not. Once again, I let myself know that this is the path I chose, and it is on me to follow through with it. After I pressed send, I stuck the note to the front door and made my way downstairs.

After we made it to the airport, I was in complete awe. The amount of henchmen to secure a safe send off for Marona was just unbelievable. It looked as if the henchmen made up twenty percent of the airports population. Marona seemed pretty happy to see me, "Arrun my boy," he called out with joy. Standing with his arms out, I was pretty sure he was expecting a hug; and a hug was exactly what I gave him as he continued to speak.

"Kid, I don't know where on Earth you came from, but if it wasn't for you I wouldn't be here right now. I could care less of how you've lived your life to this point; I've got two sons, and henceforth you are the third. I want you to get involved in all our activities. I don't usually trust someone so soon, but there's something about you."

In all honesty I was not expecting so much attention from Marona. When he said I was coming to Tamil Nadu with him I thought I would just be another one of his henchmen. A son? I did not see that coming at all; I have never had a father figure in my life. It was actually something I have always wanted, and after speaking to Marona, I actually look forward to where my choice will lead me.

After Marona spoke to me, we were ready for departure. We went through security clearance, and made way towards the gate. I was assuming that we would board a flight with many other citizens, but they had a private jet! These guys were the real deal; slowly I began progressing in thoughts. Maybe I didn't make such a bad choice? Then again I was smart enough to know not to judge this lifestyle till I see what Chennai had in store for me.

I anticipated more people joining us on the airline, but a large sum of them were only there to make sure we got on the jet safely.

"Going to be a long ride bro, it's better to get sleep," suggested Remone.

"I'll try, but it's your marijuana that's been putting me to sleep as of late," I replied.

Remone sitting across from me laughed; looking over to my right Marona grinned, as I smirked back. As the pilot spoke, I closed my eyes, in preparation of a wild ride.

Chapter 9 - A Wild Start

In the midst of a new beginning I closed my eyes to a memory of Hasini, one that I have failed to consider till now. It was of the time she took me to the place I proposed to her; I believe it was about three or four months before I proposed. I remember it because it was the first time the thought of death even crossed my mind. It was just another ordinary day, and Hasini had invited me to a place she admires a lot. Walking through the forest path she was asking me loads of random questions.

"Arrun what would you do if I died tomorrow?" She asked, putting me on the spot.

"Hasini, honestly? What sort of dumb question is that?" I asked back confused.

"Just answer it," she demanded.

"I'd probably lose it, go insane. I honestly don't know what I would do without you. Probably jut become one of those really emotional people, maybe feel like dying?"

"You love me that much," she asked.

"Yes!" I shouted.

"What are you a fruitcake," asked Hasini; the both of us laughed.

"What do you mean," I asked.

"I mean don't be a complete idiot. Would you really go to extents of throwing you're entire life away if I die? I thought the man I loved was stronger than that; I expected him to have the courage to face all odds. Arrun it's cute, it's cute that you love me so much, but please don't be one of those emotional wrecks. You have the potential to go really far in life; don't make me responsible for your downfall. If I'm gone I want you to fall in love again, and continue leading a life where you're happy!"

Intensely smiling I responded, "You thought I was serious? Of course I'd move on!"

"Jerk," Hasini's reaction was priceless; she knew I was joking though.

She would have hated seeing the way I turned out. That day, I just considered it a topic of discussion. I did not deem in the likelihood of either one of us loosing each other till we were well aged and through with life. It's quite amusing how sometimes a casual talk of possibility can end up as reality; it happens so very often without most of our notice.

This memory may have been what I needed all along; resting my eyes finally seemed possible. I needed to change; I needed to reduce my emotions and become stronger. I had to once again become the man that Hasini loved.

There was some alcohol on the flight, after a few shots I was good to sleep for a while.

"Wake up, bro wake up!" Shouted a voice.

An unexpected disturbance suddenly woke me up. I haven't slept this peacefully in months! It was Remone who disturbed my peace, all because he was bored.

"Arrun, I didn't want to disturb you but, I'm so bored man," he said.

"Why'd you have to disturb my rest? Couldn't you go talk to Marona?" I asked.

"Seriously bro? Do you want to see me get thrown off this plane? Is it so difficult for you to stay awake for a few more hours? You slept through majority of the trip man; let me remind me you, this plane ride is 23hrs long!"

I guess he was right, I mean I did sleep through majority of this trip. There was about five more hours till our arrival to Chennai, Tamil Nadu, and it would make sense for me to actually learn more about Remone. Maybe I could even get an idea of what to expect when we get there.

"Fine man you win, I'll stay up for the next few hours," I said in a displeased tone.

"So tell me Remone, how'd you get involved in all this?" I asked, curiously.

"Oh man that's a long story," he said.

"Bro, don't you think we have the time, just tell me," I urged.

"Okay, I was going to tell you. You're the one that cut me off," he said, as he prepared to share his story.

"I've been around this stuff for about ten years now. I was born in Chennai; I've never even seen my mother, apparently she split when I was born. My dad was an asshole bro; the dude beat me almost everyday. I'm not even surprised that my mother left us, I mean who would want to live with someone like him. I'd say I was about sixteen when I decided to leave home too. There was this one-day when I was trying to find food; I decided to rob one of these big scary dudes. Obviously my luck, he caught me trying to steal and beat the shit out of me. Verone Duranji, Marona's eldest son was the one who saved me. He helped me stick around and find small jobs to pay for necessities; and now they allow me to be involved in some of the more serious situations. I became a man watching the business. I think you'd like Verone, but Miran is going to be kind of hard getting used to."

"Is Miran Marona's second son," I queried; I was beginning to get curious.

"Yeah he is, and trust me bro, you do not want to get on that guys bad side. He's only a few years older than us, but the guy is scarier than the devil himself. Marona loves him; it's probably because Miran is literally the youthful version of himself. The guy doesn't give a damn about what happens after his actions. If you get in his way, you'll probably end up dead."

"So basically he's a psycho, who gets to roam free," I commented.

"Quiet bro! Marona is going to hear you," whispered Remone.

"Alright, don't worry I'll be quiet. So tell me, what kind of shit did I get myself into?"

"I know you were an engineer and all before, but you need to know that your new job is far from that. In case you don't know, you're lawless now. Just as much of dirt bag as any person you'll be meeting in the next few hours. Society never liked us, but they don't understand that we need to be criminals to survive. If we don't resort to this we'd probably be a panhandler, roaming the streets asking stuck up rich people for coin. With this job we're able to earn more money than the average man. You're going to be involved in drug trafficking, extortion, kidnapping, assassinations, and the business world politics. You may not like it, but I think you'll get the hang of it."

"Sounds pretty serious, but I'm not doing it for the money," I replied.

"Why would you want to be a criminal then," asked Remone.

"I don't know; as of late life just feels really empty, I need a thrill. That's what I used to enjoy about life, the rush feeling. It made me feel alive; I want it again, I don't want to wake up every morning and feel death dragging me down."

"I can't nail a character assessment on you bro. At first I thought you were some depressed dude, and then you come save the day, after that you topped it off with a murder, and now this. I think this can be the beginning of a great friendship."

Remone was right, this could be the start of a great friendship. Maybe I was just quick on the trigger, judging him. He is actually a really cool guy; he had to be a criminal to survive, because life did not allow him to go in any other direction.

We continued to trade stories of our lives over the last few hours of travel. I still refrained from speaking about Hasini, even though she did come up in the conversation here and there.

It took a days travel for us to reach our destination, but looking out the window I could see the large landmass that holds my future. I didn't know how to feel about it; I was born in Chennai, but I haven't been back since Sarah adopted me. The death of my parents led to my departure, and now murder is what brought me back; death has been my only true companion.

As we got set for landing I felt my mind ease a little more. It felt amazing; after months of sheer torture to my thoughts, I finally had a sense of relief. Hasini will always be the one that got away, but its time for me to move on and venture into what life has in store for me next.

Stepping out the private airline, I was expecting a lot of men for an escort to the Duranji residence. Although to my surprise that was not the case, there were actually just two vehicles with a driver in each. Walking down the flight of stairs I was confused; this is it? I thought Marona Duranji was a big deal; and all he gets is a measly driver for a pick up? The vehicles were nice though, two black Range Rovers; I did not expect Chennai to be so modern. Then again, I guess being an international criminal pays a little more than what the average man makes.

"Welcome to my world kid," whispered Marona. As usual I just replied back with a smile. I really did not know how to talk to the guy, its not that I was scared of him but he hasn't lived up to that acclaimed name of his just yet. It just keeps me speculating of what the hype is about. Remone and I watched as the two henchmen whom accompanied us on our journey loaded the luggage. The henchmen both join Marona, in the first SUV. I was joined by Remone in the second; following the other vehicle, in what was said to be an hour-long drive.

Twenty minutes into the ride I could not help but find myself in awe; Chennai is far more beautiful and developed than I imagined. When you're raised in a westernized country its hard to consider the fact that the rest of the world develops with time; however the level of visible poverty is not a pleasant sight. As I continued to stare in amazement, I was still curious of how someone of Marona's standards only had two men present for his arrival.

"Hey Remone, does the driver understand English," I whispered.

"No, Why?" Questioned Remone.

"I've been curious about this since we got off the jet; why is it that there were only two cars to pick up Marona? Like the guy was almost killed a few nights ago, shouldn't there be more protection? We don't even know who planned the attack on him."

"Arrun, my friend. You need to understand that Chennai is the Duranji district; there is no one on the radar who is gutsy enough to attempt an empire takedown."

The hype truly never fades; with every passing moment Marona's name is mentioned, his praise reaches a new level. I for one think that they are way to in over their heads. Look at me; just a few months back I thought I had my life all figured out, but my story had other twists in store. Marona could be the world's biggest criminal, but at the end of the day, he dies; like every other man.

As I continued to glance through the window, admiring my new unfamiliar setting I noticed a red vehicle racing by. The men in the vehicle were masked; within a blink of an eye I was witness to Marona's vehicle heating under heavy fire. As our driver slammed the break, I felt the pressure of the seat belt surge against my chest. Remone was quick to react; he reached over the seat into the trunk grabbing two sub-machine guns, and as we ducked our body behind the seat he quickly showed me how to use the gun. There was a calm relief running through my body, and the emotionless soul I've had the past few months was beginning to get the best of me. I closed my eyes, and the sounds around me drifted seemingly slow. Remone had taken cover behind the left passenger door; I could hear him desperately crying out my name for support.

Opening my door, I watched as our elderly driver attempted to flee. His attempt fell short as he received an immediate piercing bullet to his head. Closing the door behind me I started walking towards the masked men, with a gun in my hand, blazing. Without any training, I really just fired at will; looking forward in the direction of Marona's vehicle I noticed that the henchmen had already taken down a few of the masked men. Unfortunately for them they're pure flesh wasn't bulletproof; I tried shooting down the surrounding masked individuals but, the henchmen fell to their deaths.

I could hear Remone calling out to me, pleading to take cover behind the SUV. I ignored him, continuously pacing towards Marona's Range Rover; at this point I did not even know if Marona was alive, but he called me his son. Emptying my clip, I brought down three of the unidentified men; only one remained. Through the tinted rear window I could see movement; it was Marona! He was fine, but if I didn't think quickly, the last remaining foe would have surely got him. Dropping the empty gun to the ground I began to sprint in the direction of Marona's vehicle; "ARRUN! Watch out," Remone shouted. I was in a clear aim for the masked man; he could end my life right there, or maybe he'll miss. I was willing to take my chance with him; racing straight for the man, I heard the bursts of rapid fire.

Remone managed to take down the last man; turning in his direction I playfully said, "Nice shot bro," he didn't seem to be pleased with my methods. Marona stepped out of his vehicle, unharmed. He was furious; it was probably his disbelief that someone actually tried to take him out. But the poor soul Remone shot didn't die just yet; Marona walked over and unmasked the covert man. "Tell me who sent you, and maybe you'll live to see another day," he whispered. "Shekhar Khan," responded the man in hopes of being spared, but sparing the man who tried to kill him was the last of Marona's belief. With mighty force Marona clomped down into the mans face, merely using his foot.

"Remone! Call one of those idiots to come pick us up," ordered a furious

Marona.

I stood beside Remone as he made the call, and before you knew it there were vehicles hammering in left and right. Seeing the amount of back up rolling in I could not stop but wonder why these fools couldn't just be with us in the first place. The lives of the innocent drivers could have been spared; I wonder who's going to support their families now.

"Arrun! Come over here, I want you to meet some people," called out Marona.

I began walking towards Marona, and I watched as he began gathering all his men in a crowd. As I stood side by side with him he began to speak; the way everyone stood around him, you would think he was a politician or something.

> "I am your king, there is no denying that; nor will there ever be any change in that. Starting today along with Verone and Miran, you'll be listening to the orders of Arrun, my third son. He's saved my life on two occasions now; something you idiots should've been doing. While were talking about that, would anyone of you idiots like to explain to me why the these two dead henchmen were sent to protect me?"

"Remone, saved your life too," I interrupted.

Marona and the other men immediately turned their head in my direction. "Remone's the one who shot down the last man," I said calmly; I don't think these guys respect Remone enough to be such a big piece of their kingdom, and it bothered me. Remone running next to me spoke, "Sorry Marona, I don't think he meant to interrupt you." I stood confused; I don't understand why he watched as I was given all the credit.

"Are you serious, with all this bullshit," intruded a voice in the crowds.

"Verone and I are you only sons. You bring some pampered kid from Canada and throw him in to the deep waters, thinking he could swim? You're getting too old pops, allowing some little bitch to speak up to you. Oh look the bitch and our pet dog Remone saved the day. Get back on the plane and ship your ass back to Canada little one, this game is for the big kids."

Through the crowd of men walked forth Miran, with an attitude to complement what Remone vouched. I did not appreciate a single word that came out of his mouth; I did not come here to be another one of their pets. Stepping eye to eye with the animal, I replied, "You call Remone the dog, but you're the one barking."

"What did you say to me?" Shouted Miran.

"What are you deaf," I questioned.

The heat was rising; I noticed that I wasn't off to a great start at making friends. Like statues we stood face to face, waiting for the other to instigate something. "Both of you, get yourselves together," said Marona as he attempted to break the tension. He ordered everyone to head back into the cars and make way to the Duranji residence.

I rode in the same vehicle as Marona, Remone and Verone. From what Remone told me on the flight I knew that he was closer to Verone, in contrast to the rest of the family.

"Arrun, you sure know how to make an introduction don't you," asked Verone.

I returned to my ritual of replying with a smile once again; Remone sat next to me, without words. Once we were near the Duranji residence, I went back to staring out the window with astonishment. I could not comprehend whether I looking out at reality; I knew that Marona is rich, and titles himself as king, but this guy was serious. He did not live in some ordinary house, it looked like a palace, and the amount of land it covered was beyond what I have ever seen.

By the time we got to the residence, I realized that the confrontation between Miran and I had already reached the rest of the henchmen. I felt like a movie star considering all the attention I was getting, it was actually quiet annoying. Nudging me, Remone whispered, "Bro are you for real? Where the hell did you get the balls?" I was actually amused at Remone's disbelief; "We're a man of our own, we aren't meant to be controlled by another. Remember that," I replied. I noticed that Miran didn't return back to the residence as the rest of did.

"Arrun, why don't you go eat something, while someone gets a room ready for you," suggested Marona.

I kindly refused; I already had told Remone that I'd live with him and a few others we'd be working with.

"He can stay with me Marona," suggested Remone.

"Yeah, it would be preferable if I stay with someone I already know," I supported.

"Alright kid, suit yourself. It's probably for the best anyway, seeing how you and Miran have already started getting along so well. Go there and get some rest, we've got some serious work to get down to tomorrow. Remone, keep a good eye on this solider; he seems to be a fierce one. By the way, swing by Raja's place and get Arrun acquainted with him."

"Will do," responded Remone.

Chapter 10 - Let The Games Begin

Back on the road, I asked Remone about this Raja character. "Filling you in on everything is going to be a part-time job," he said sarcastically.

"Raja Krishnamurthy is Marona's right hand. Seriously, this guy has been with Marona from the get go. No one but Raja knows the complete story of how Marona managed to build the colossal empire that he is. When you see Raja you're going to have a really hard time believing that this guy is involved in any criminal activity; he's the purest definition of innocence in disguise. He's a lot older now, so he takes care of the business portions accompanied by Verone. Although his focus is in the business world, his opinions in Marona's decisions still remain very crucial."

Raja's home wasn't so far from the Duranji residence; we were in Raja's driveway within a short span of ten minutes. These guys cease to amaze me; Marona's place was a palace but Raja's home is hardly a step down. Being someone who was raised in North America, I found it really hard to believe that some of the housing in this part of the world exceeded what I was used to.

Getting out of the SUV, Remone pointed out Raja who was accompanied by a few other classy looking men. Remone was not kidding when he said that I would be in disbelief; Raja was actually quiet short, with slicked black hair, and glasses. He just did not fit the description of someone who would be involved in criminal activities. "You've got to be kidding me," I said, as Remone smiled back. Raja must have known that we were coming; the moment he saw us, he left his company and approached us.

"You must be the infamous Arrun that everyone has been talking about," said Raja.

Seriously? How on earth is the news spreading so fast, I feel like I'm surrounded by a bunch of gossip girls trying to act like tough men. Just as I have grown so accustomed to, I responded to Raja with a smile. "If you need any money, be sure to swing by and ask me," he said. At this point, replying with my fake smile, started to become an automatic response, but I would much rather throw them a smile than having to actually converse with them.

"By the way, what's your full name," Raja asked.

"Arrun Durai," I responded.

"Alright Arrun, I don't want to hold onto you and Remone the whole day. Take the day to get acquainted and comfortable to your new environment. I'll probably be seeing you both tomorrow morning at the meeting."

I was actually glad to be able to leave; I didn't want to stick around with the tiny man the entire day. The heat is one thing that I am going to have a hard time tolerating. Living in Canada we did have warm summers, but India was just too hectic. Besides, I have already had an eventful day, and some rest is what I needed. Especially because tomorrow would not be a walk in the park, of course considering the day I had today.

~

On the way over to Remone's place, he let me know that we would be living with three other guys. Thambi, who is apparently an overgrown, overweight twenty-five year old; Sethu the odd ball, a twenty-seven year old who is always down for anything and everything; and Renny, the twenty-seven year old who is the funny guy that turns serious according to the situation.

For guys who are criminals for a living, these guys knew how to live a fancy lifestyle. Even those working under Marona, lived in nice places. Parking the SUV, Remone pointed out to me that it was Renny who was standing outside having a smoke. Stepping out of the vehicle I gave him a head nod. "Arrun bro, a nod? That's all I get, give me a hug brother," yelled Renny.

"I guess you already know who I am?" I asked.

"Know you? You're like the only unexpected event we've seen happen in years. All of us were there earlier today when you got into a dispute with Miran. You're one badass man! Never thought anyone would have the guts to speak back to anyone in the Duranji family. Also it's pretty clear that you've really impressed Marona, seeing how you're still alive after speaking up to his favorite son."

"Someone had to let him know right?" I questioned.

"Well nobody who values their life would," replied Renny.

He was right, someone who valued their life would not have done half the things I did over the past few days. Maybe I didn't value my life, or maybe I am still searching for a life to value.

I only brought a luggage of clothes and some cash over from Toronto; walking through the front door, I stood eye to eye with a hippo! I did not need to ask Remone to know which of the three I was looking at. Thambi was cramming down some chicken when I saw him. The dude smiled back at me while holding a piece of chicken in his hands. "Want some," he questioned. I stood steady for a brief moment just staring at him; a second later dropping my luggage to the floor I began to laugh uncontrollably; it felt great. I couldn't remember the last time I laughed; Thambi translates to little brother in Tamil, but I knew I was going to have a hard time calling him that. Remone and Renny walk in curious as to what had me laughing so hard. The moment they turned through the doors, they too joined in laughing intensely; soon after even Thambi joined us.

The only person left to meet was Sethu, the odd ball. Remone was in Toronto for some time prior to coming back to India with me; he spent some time catching up with Thambi while Renny showed me my room. Walking up the stairs I got a whiff of a familiar smell.

"Is someone smoking up?" I asked.

"Probably Sethu," responded Renny.

Coming here for a new beginning, smoking marijuana was definitely something I wanted to keep out of the picture. I need to create myself a stronger mentality; I don't want to rely on a drug to help me forget memories. Observing myself over the last few days I know there has been change in my behavior. Things were beginning to look brighter; I am able to sleep, laugh, and communicate with others. I may never find the person I used to be, but maybe I could recreate myself.

Renny knocked on Sethu's door so I can meet him. Sethu opened his door with a joint between his lips. "What's up bro," asked Sethu lending his hand out as a gesture of friendship. Shaking his hand, I was wondering why Remone called him the odd one. He smiled, and slowly stepped back behind his door and closed it.

"Well, that was weird," I said

"That's Sethu for you, you'll get used to it," responded Renny.

Renny showed me my room before heading back downstairs; settling in I actually liked this place. In my dark room I took a seat, everything I needed was right there for me. Although there was one factor that needed a change, the blinds were closed, and it was time for change. I can't be living in the dark anymore; pulling the curtains, I watched as the room began to flood with light, lights of new life.

Since our arrival time flew, it would be the appropriate time for me to get some rest. With all that happened throughout the day, I knew that I should be expecting some wild things tomorrow. The new life I began today is not one that everyone often dreams of, but I think it's growing on me.

Chapter 11 - Hostage

It was fairly early when I went to bed yesterday evening; the time now is five in the morning and I am pretty sure the rest of the guys are asleep right now. My coffee and cigarette routine is not one to stop so easily; so I made my way down to the kitchen to get myself a cup. Coming down the stairs, I turned to the right in direction of the kitchen to find Sethu awake, sitting at the dining table rolling another joint.

"Bro did you even sleep," I asked.

"Yeah, why do you think I closed the door on you yesterday," he said.

"Couldn't you just say, you were going to sleep," I questioned.

"What's the fun in that," he responded.

What's the fun in that? What is that even supposed to mean, I stood there questioning myself. I was starting to realize why he is supposedly the weird one.

"I'm going to make some coffee, do you want some," I asked.

"No, but I wouldn't mind it if you poor me a shot," he said.

"Bro! It's five in the morning! Is everything good," I inquired.

"What? A guy can't drink in the morning? Not everyone who drinks is a complete mess. I just like to start my day off with a little buzz. Reality is just too boring, a hit from my joint and a shot of whisky and I'll be buzzed the entire morning. Besides it helps when you're a criminal, with all the shit you're asked to do."

"Say no more brother, I got you," I responded as I headed into the kitchen to make the coffee and poor a shot for Sethu. By the time I had both in hand, he was already at the top of the house. The house is pretty awesome seeing how we're able to go over to the flat surfaced rooftop and have a great view of the entire city. It was quite amazing because it was the first time I was able to see it myself; Remone mentioned the view as we were on our way to the house, but I didn't expect it to be stunning.

"Pretty amazing, isn't it" asked Sethu as he extended out his hand for the shot of whisky. "Breathtaking," I responded placing a smoke between my lips. We both stood staring out into the open without a word, at peace. Sometimes you forget how big the world is, and you think it's hard to find opportunities. Standing in another part of the world you start to think that there actually is a possibility to live more than one life in an existence.

Breaking our silence was the ringing of Sethu's phone. It was from the Duranji residence; they wanted for us to meet up at their place in an hour's time. "Let's see what today has in store for us, shall we," said Sethu. He headed back down to wake up the rest of the guys as I sat against the edge of the house looking out into the city. I've never been such a religious person; nevertheless I do often find myself speaking to Pillayar, Lord Ganesha, as he's often referred to in hopes of him hearing.

"I often speak to you in hopes of you hearing my cries. I've always preferred to deal with things on my own; and even though I often say I don't believe in god I find it necessary to turn to you in my times of need. Is it wrong? Is it wrong, that I only turn to you when I've got a problem? As humans we turn to people we trust in times of need, isn't that what I'm doing with you? If god did put humans on this planet, this choice was bound by you, is it not? I've often been thankful for the world I lived in, great people, and a great job, with something exciting in roads ahead. Although in recent times, my life has tumbled down. Sarah went to great extents to learn about Hinduism for me to have knowledge of my inherited religion. One thing I remember her telling me is that you are the overcomer of obstacles. Is that why you brought me to India? Did you crash my world, to build another? Show me another road, please god show me something."

"Arrun, its time to leave," said Remone, standing at the stairs leading to the rooftop.

"Cool, I'll be down just now," I replied.

~

By the time we made it to Marona's house many of the men were already there. Walking into the palace of residency, I was still in amazement; the architectural work was astonishing. Raja and Verone were both right at the entrance to greet us. I even saw Miran surrounded by some of his friends; his face said it all; he was not happy with my presence. Walking down the stairs, Marona let us know of what had occurred, and the plan for what will happen next.

"As most of you know Shekhar Khan thought that he could kill me earlier yesterday. Last night a little birdy came over to let me know that Shekhar Khan apparently has a little deal with the Tamil Nadu Police Commissioner, Muthumaran Selvaraj. The plan is set so that I'm out of the picture, clearing criminal activities in Tamil Nadu. We can't let that happen now can we? Around 2am last night we kidnapped Muthumaran's loving daughter, Nilani Selvaraj. We've kept her hostage at a brothel house a few miles from here. Arrun, I want you and your group of guys to go there and keep watch. There shouldn't be any problems, there aren't many who know the whereabouts; just keep an eye on her. "

Miran didn't seem to like the idea of Marona giving me the

responsibilities; he rushed out the door knocking over objects in sight. I guess he might have taken offence to it, but I could care less of what he thinks. "Alright, let him act like a little girl," said Marona. Some of the men were actually laughing at Marona's joke, even though they knew of Miran's attitude. Maybe they lost fear in him, watching an outsider like myself come into the picture to face him.

There was no need for us to stick around after Marona filled us in; causally waving to Marona I walked out the door as Remone, Renny, Sethu and Thambi followed. As I got into the front passenger seat, Thambi said, "Miran seemed to be really pissed of brother."

"Am I supposed to be scared of him? He's just like you and me," I responded.

"Yes! You should be scared, the guys a psycho," said Remone.

It was pretty obvious that everyone believed for me to be Miran's primary target, even amidst all the occurring problems. I didn't really see the need to care for him, after all Hasini's death was surely a greater problem for me to deal with. Although the strange happenings over the past few days have got me wondering if I am moving on.

On pace to the brothel I just stared at my legs, completely lost in thoughts. It was weird; I could not understand how I went from losing myself months ago to the verge of forgetting. I guess it makes sense, as humans we can never live every second of our lives feeling the same emotion. Every second changes us; the unbearable will become a thing of the past, as life presents new opportunities and challenges. Hasini will be the most unforgettable person in my life, but life must go on.

Life must go on, and I am realizing that now. Yet I do not feel regret for leaving everything back in Toronto. I had a life many people would kill for, but I prefer the life I have started to build here. I don't know how long it will last, but as of now this is exactly where I want to be.

"Arrun, you got some nice legs, I get why you can't stop staring at them," said Renny laughing hysterically. "Shut up bro," I responded as I smiled; I often forget how it must look to others while I get absorbed in thoughts. Remone turned left into an off road trail, and we drove for another fifteen minutes before reaching the brothel. The place did not really seem like a brothel to be honest; I had all these ideas as for what I should be expecting, but all expectations were failed. I guess, I just thought of it to be similar to what I would see in movies. The house itself seemed pretty nice, painted all white, with a numerous amount of windows. The gardening in front of the house was so exquisite that I was in complete denial to call the place a brothel. There were a few luxurious cars that were parked up at the side of the house. It could explain why the house itself looked so nice; the place was probably a brothel for high-end rollers.

Walking into the brothel, I wasn't sure of what to expect. The moment we walked through the door the five us just stood in awe as our jaws dropped. So many beautiful girls; it is a shame that they have to resort to prostitution for means of income. I looked to my left and right as I stood in the middle of us five, the excitement on the faces of the guys was as if they won the lotto. As the female hosts approached us they were generally really touchy.

"How can we help you boys today," asked one of the girls.

"We're here on business, Marona sent us," I replied.

"Oh the crying girl upstairs," she asked.

"Nilani?" I asked for confirmation.

"Yeah, she's right up the stairs; two doors to your left," she replied.

Turning to my friends I let them know it was fine if they wanted to "hang out" with some of the girls. It was just one girl; she can't be so much trouble. The guys didn't even think twice, they agreed to my proposal and went their ways with the girls. The funniest of the four was Thambi, who left with two girls. As I began walking up the flight of stairs, Remone called out my name. "Here keep this gun," he said; there was no point in me having it, but I took it anyway.

Nilani was out cold as I walked into the dark room, I noticed that her plate of food and water reminded untouched. Walking next to her, I took a seat on the bed as I attempted to wake her up. I didn't want to tap her on the shoulder, she might think that I had come here with wrong intentions; we were in a brothel after all. Simply saying, "wake up," didn't work; I had no other option but to dump the bottle of water on her face. She woke with fear; I turned completely drawn to her eyes opening wide as tears dropped like rapid tides.

"Please don't do anything to me! Can I go home, I don't know what I did! Is it money that you want? You can call my dad, he's the Tamil Nadu Police Commissioner; he'll give you whatever you want. This place gives me the creeps, please take me home; I'll let my dad know not press charges. Are you going to rape me, I'm not like the rest of the girls in this house; I'm not a prostitute"

"Could you shut up? I'm not going to rape you! You'll just have to stick around here for a few days at most. Learn to eat your food, cause you aren't going home anytime soon."

She glared at me for a brief moment before giving a nice spit to my white t-shirt. Surprisingly I felt no bit of anger towards her; instead I took grasp of her hand and used it to wipe her spit.

"That is gross," she screamed.

"What? It's your spit," I replied.

Her displeasure of my presence reminded me of something similar to my first conversation with Hasini at the bar in the Dominican. I guess I was never bound to have a nice first meeting with attractive girls. Nilani was just as beautiful as Hasini; though their similarities were limited. Her long tied up hair, absorbing brown eyes, and beautiful cheekbones made her quite the attractive girl. "Can you stop staring at me, it's kind of creepy," she said. There was still a weird feeling about Nilani that reminded me of Hasini. "Sorry, you just had me thinking of someone I knew," I replied.

I continuously asked her to eat and she just stared at me like I had something on my face.

"How am I supposed to eat with my hands tied up," she asked.

"I can't untie your hands, wouldn't want you to do anything dumb," I said.

"Then feed me," she suggested.

"Seriously? Are you cool with that," I questioned.

"How else am I supposed to eat you idiot," she retorted.

While feeding her she began to ask questions of why she's being held hostage. I really should've just left her remain asleep.

"Why are you being so nice? Are you trying to play nice? I know about people like you, don't start thinking for one second that I'm not aware of your true intentions. I don't even know who you are; what's you name?

Why am I here? I think you've got the wrong girl, I don't get why I'd be here."

"Wow, could you just slow down for a bit. My name is Arrun, and I work for Marona Duranji. Your father is making deals with some really bad people to kill my boss; and you're only here for a few days to send him a message. Don't worry, no harms going to come your way as long as I'm around. Now eat your food so I can leave for a smoke."

She was starting to cooperate a bit more. After she finished eating, I found it to be an appropriate time to move out for a quick smoke. I let her know that I'll be stepping out to the balcony around the corner for a brief moment. "Arrun, I guess you're alright," said Nilani, as I was walking towards the door. "Stay awake, I'll come back and talk to you for a bit," I said closing the door behind me.

~

I stood over the balcony to notice another one of Marona's Range Rovers to be parked in front of the house. I guess he sent over a few more henchmen in case something was to have happened. I guess you can never take too many precautions, especially considering the event that took place yesterday.

Moments later I heard a loud cry for help, it was coming from inside the house. Tossing my smoke over the balcony edge, I rushed inside. The scream was coming from the room we were keeping Nilani in. I tried turning the doorknob, but it was locked from inside. "Arrun, Arrun," screamed Nilani from inside. I took a step back, and aimed at a spot beside the doorknob. With full force I kicked open the door to see Miran trying to force himself on Nilani.

Grabbing Miran by the shoulder I ordered him to let Nilani go. "Get off me you piece of shit," he said turning towards me. He threw a punch straight to the right side of my jaw. "Is that all you got," I asked stepping back towards him. "Do you a favor and step out till I'm done here," he said. I continued to stand in front of Miran, I did not say a word waiting for him to try and hit me once more. Miran attempted to swing a second punch, but this time I saw it coming. Quickly ducking, I dodged his punch; I then swung a punch straight to his chest. He had a momentary drop in breath; taking advantage of the situation I swung a solid punch to his nose, and as blood began to flow down his face I gave him a lateral stomp to the side of his left kneecap. The moment he dropped to the floor I stood over him, as my left hand grasped his shirt, my right arm swung ruthlessly to the right side of his face. I've never felt anger like this before; I didn't want to stop.

"Arrun! Stop! You're going to kill him, stop," pleaded Nilani.

Sethu must have heard the screaming as well, rushing into the room he tackled me to ground. I'm sure I could've beat Miran to death at the rate I was hitting him. I didn't want to allow him to live; his existence is not needed. Sadly he will live, but I was glad that he would be living with a few broken bones. "You have to control yourself," said Sethu, as he checked Miran.

"He tried to rape her, what was I supposed to do allow him," I countered.

"Yeah! Who cares about her? She's a nobody," said Sethu.

"I care, I'm not going to just let him do shit like that," I responded.

Turning over to Nilani, I untied both ropes arresting her arms and legs. "Don't run," I commanded, as she stood quietly. "What are you doing Arrun," probed Sethu.

"I'm taking her out to the balcony, I didn't finish my smoke," I replied.

Walking out the door, I held Nilani's arm for precaution. We turned left and walked over to the balcony where I lit another cigarette. Looking over at Nilani I said, "Don't think about jumping, you wont make it." Smiling at her, I turned to look out over the balcony, with a vast amount of land in sight. In the distance the city is nowhere in sight; these guys were pretty smart to place a brothel way out here.

"Thank you Arrun," said Nilani.

"For what," I questioned.

"I've never been so scared in my life, thank you for caring," she responded.

"Look, I didn't come into the room because I cared about you. Why should I? You aren't my mother, wife, sister, or girlfriend; I don't need to care about you. I just don't like that guy. Besides I have a few women in my life that mean the world to me. I wouldn't have spared a sick bastard like Miran, for laying a finger on them."

"Gosh Arrun, you don't need to be so rude about it," she retorted.

"It is, what it is," I said.

"If you don't mind me asking, where did you learn to fight like that? It was like watching a scene from a Bruce Lee movie."

"I learned "Mixed Martial Arts" sometime back; I think it was when I was in high school? Sarah was the one who forced it on me; she thought I needed to learn to defend myself. I used to get into many fights during those times, and it felt great cause I actually knew how to fight."

Nilani's face explained the confusion she was in. I forgot how high school was labeled otherwise in India. A name like Sarah was probably not tossed around commonly either.

"I was raised in Canada, Sarah adopted me when I was just a toddler," I said, in hopes of clearing her confusion. Although her expressions showed otherwise, she seemed to be more puzzled than ever. "Why on Earth are you here; doing this for a living," she questioned. I wanted to tell her; I usually always want to tell people of my reasoning, but I always hold back. "It's a long story," I responded in hope that she'd just let it drop.

"I'm going to be here for a few days, I think you've got time," she replied. Nilani seemed determined to know what my story actually was. Of all the people I've met in recent events, I felt more comfortable saying it to her. Seeing how I probably wont have to come across her ever again, it would be great to just know that someone else in the world knows my entire story.

> "I was born in Chennai, but raised in Canada. My parents were murdered when I was just a few months old, and it was Sarah who adopted and gave me a meaningful life. Went through schooling there, I graduated and found a job as a software engineer at some big time company. I have five siblings and…"

I was in the midst of explaining my story when I heard the roaring of engines coming from the direction we first arrived. Seconds later, I watched as six vehicles full of unfamiliar faces pulled in with weapons in arm. They were not any of our men; I took out the gun I had holstered at my side, in case of a sudden interaction. "Nilani, stay down," I ordered as I stood waiting for someone to spot me. It didn't take them too long to make first contact. "Did Marona send you guys," I investigated, from the top floor. "Shekhar Khan," one replied as they started to fire at will. Taking immediate cover next to Nilani, I opened the balcony door, dragging her in with me.

Holding Nilani by the wrist I was heading back downstairs to regroup with the guys when I remembered that Sethu was still attending to

Miran. Running past the room I stopped to see if they were still there. "Sethu, we need to go! Bring Miran with you," I shouted. "He's too heavy, I need your help," he responded; I had no choice but to assist him. I trusted that Nilani would not run, and she didn't do so either as we helped Miran down the stairs. We placed him on the couch, as we regrouped with the other guys. In the immediate seconds later, three men stormed through the door. I was able to shoot down two of the three, as Sethu took out the final one.

"They're still out there, a lot more of them," I said

"Then this is our chance to try and make moves from here," recommend Remone.

"There's a back door, it's our best chance," mentioned Renny.

Nilani held tight to my arm, I could see the fear she was in. "Thambi, help me pick up Miran," shouted Sethu. As the both of them helped Miran, Remone and Renny led the way through the back door. We walked around the back: I checked over the side of the house to see how many people stood between the vehicle and us.

"Alright, there are seven of them outside the house. The rest of them are probably raiding the house right now. I don't think we have much time before they notice a back door, so we need to move quickly! Remone, you and I are going to take that first SUV with Nilani. We'll take out as many of them as we can on our way to the vehicle, but Renny you'll have to help us from here. Then the three of you can take the second vehicle

and take Miran to a hospital."

"Sounds good," said Renny, while the rest of the guys nodded. "Nilani, follow us! Don't stop," I instructed. Executing by force I took out two more men; Remone cleared another three, while Renny took care of the remaining two. I got into the driver seat of the first vehicle as we were faced with more gunfire; men were rushing out from within the house. "Arrun," called out Thambi as he held grasp of a propane tank. "Shoot it," he shouted as he rolled it in direction of the incoming men. I waited to make sure all the guys were safely in the vehicles before firing a final bullet at the tank. BANG! I watched as the explosion incinerated the few men along with the front of the brothel. "That's what I'm talking about," cheered Remone. Firing guns in the air we drove off, cursing at will as we saw the remaining few men run to the front of the house in shock.

"What now, where are we taking Nilani" asked Remone as we watched the others turn in direction of the hospital.

"We're taking her to her house," I replied.

"What? Did you get hit in the head or something? What are we going to tell Marona? I've been listening to a few of your wild ideas now, but this is the worst of them all. Why don't you just ask one of us to kill you? Because it seems like you just do things to die."

"Calm down bro, I don't plan on dying till death comes and gets me. I just think it's better if she goes home now. Think about it, Shekhar Khan is supposedly working with the commissioner, but the way his men came *firing they could've killed her as well. Which means, the commissioner probably didn't know of this plan. He'll probably withdraw from their so called deal; leaving Shekhar Khan to be our only problem."*

"Alright bro, fuck! I can't believe I'm actually listening to you again," said Remone

"Trust me brother, you have to," I responded smiling.

Looking in the rear-view mirror, I watched Nilani, as she seemed to look disappointed. I did not want to ask her if anything was wrong; I just wanted to drop her off and end this little issue once and for all. Though she remained quiet for majority of the ride, she guided us to her house when needed. Once we arrived at her house, I parked the vehicle a short distance from the front gates.

"Remone, stay in the car. I don't know how this will go; if this ends badly I want you to drive off. Don't think twice, this is my plan and I'll deal with the situation. Nilani come, you're my ticket in and out. Don't fail me."

"Arrun, are you crazy? I'm coming," countered Remone.

"Shut up, and listen to me!" I shouted.

"Nilani, I'm going to hold a gun to your head, but I wont shoot," I promised.

I held a gun to Nilani's head as I walked through the front gates. "Muthumaran," I yelled out, as I stood waiting for the commissioner's presence. Walking through the front door was Nilani's father in tears upon seeing his daughter. "Let her go," he pleaded. Muthumaran, the Police Commissioner of Tamil Nadu in tears, proof of how great a weakness a parents love is.

> "I could shoot her right here, but I need her to ensure my safety. Remone, drive a bit forward. Muthumaran, I'm going to let your daughter go but I need to alert you of a little situation. You're dancing with the wrong person; you need to avoid that relationship with Shekhar Khan. Your daughter could have died today because his actions. We're the reason why she's alive, withdraw from your deal before we actually hurt Nilani."

"I will, I will. Please let her go," he pleaded.

"Nilani go," I said, giving her a little shove on the shoulder. Aiming my gun to her head, I walked back slowly towards the SUV door. Opening the vehicle door, I noticed Nilani enthused to run into her father's arms. However she turned to look at me, and for some odd reason her face seemed to be drowned in disappointment; it bothered me.

Chapter 12 - Making Amends

I haven't gotten much sleep since yesterdays incident. I haven't even got the time to go over to the Duranji residence to seek punishment; well assuming they weren't pleased with actions. Instead, I have been practicing my shot at an abandoned warehouse; I've come to notice that gun handling is a must. I don't want to be that one guy who is wasting bullets, shooting into space.

Remone accompanied me half way through, and he told me that I have become a fine shot. I guess that's what happens when you spend an entire day practicing. Although the compliments did not last too long, soon he began pestering me with questions of how I will explain things to Marona. To be honest I didn't know how to explain myself either. I mean, Miran now has a fractured leg and nose; I even let Nilani return home in peace. My intentions were right, and I do not doubt it at all, but I don't know if they will understand my true intentions.

"We have to go over to Marona's," said Remone.

I could have avoided it for a bit longer, but it was probably best if I don't evade this problem. Remone drove, as I started preparing for every possible scenario. Remone mentioned that there wasn't any form of hostility when Verone spoke to him over the phone; which put my mind at ease. Upon reaching the house, I noticed that most henchmen were starting to get more familiar to me. A lot of them simply nodded their head, which is usually a form of acknowledgement.

Verone was already outside; I assume he was giving a job to the henchmen. Stopping me in my tracks he said," Have a seat inside, I'll get father." As Remone mentioned, there wasn't any noticeable intimidation in Verone's tone. I really didn't need to fear for anything to go wrong, and I was right as I saw Marona approach me with a huge smile. Getting up from the couch, I was the recipient of a tight hug.

"My son, my son," he exclaimed.

"You aren't mad at me?" I asked.

"Arrun, why would I be upset with you? Because of you the commissioner has decided to cut ties with Khan! I don't care how you did it, but you got the job done and that's all that matters. Impressive kid, you just came and you've already made a significant impact on the empire. As for the situation between you and Miran; you'll have to deal with that on your own."

"Where is Miran," I asked with great hesitation. It makes sense for us to make a stronger relationship, especially with outsiders wanting the empire to fall. If we can resolve our issues, it will benefit all of us. Maybe I will have to come down a little bit; but knowing Miran, he is just going to be furious with me. Marona looked in direction of the room to the right; I understood that he must be in there.

Peaking into the room I noticed Miran lying down in his bed, with a brace over his left knee, a few stiches and a bandaged nose. I hated the guy, but watching anyone in such a condition is hard; knowing that I was responsible did not help either. To my disbelief Miran gestured me to come closer; I was expecting a lot more anger, but he seemed rather cool. "Thank you," he whispered as I stepped closed. Pure confusion ran through my mind. I was responsible for his state, yet he wants to thank me?

"You did the right thing, you made the right choice by stopping me. I get that you had to hit me; what I appreciate more was you saving me. You could have easily just let me bleed out, or even get shot down by one of Khans men, but you didn't. You actually helped me get out of that place and get medical attention. I'm indebted to you. I also heard of you getting the commissioner off our case; I guess you're alright."

I could not believe that it was Miran speaking; everything seemed so out of character. I didn't want to trust him, but he actually seemed like he was being true to the words that came out of his mouth. I thought I was the one that had to come down to make this relationship work, but he made things a lot easier. Yet there was still a slight tension and pride that stopped me from actually uttering a word to Miran, although I did give him nod to acknowledge the words that came from his mouth.

When I came out the door I bumped into Thambi, knocking over his plate of food. "Sorry brother," I said, desperately attempting to hold back laughter. The poor guy looked as if he just went through a bad break up, the way he stared down at the plate of food all over the floor.

"It's okay, is everything cool between you and Miran," he questioned.

"Yeah, it's all good," I responded; I noticed smiles across the faces of individuals around the room. I guess everyone was hoping for us to eventually get along. Our bad blood was just holding the empire from growing any further; it was right to make amends.

It was great that we made amends and all, but what mattered more was the fact that Khan is still out planning the next hit. I was able to catch both Verone and Marona at once. "I need to talk to the both of you," I demanded; and as they gave me their undivided attention I had to voice what had to be done.

"We can't just sit around and do nothing! Marona, from the moment we set foot on ground, Khan has attempted a hit. He wants you dead, and he has made it clear on two occasions; I'm pretty sure the whole situation in Toronto was his doing as well. If we don't take initiative and send a message soon, he'll surely get us all. Marona, I don't understand how you've remained so calm after all that has happened. Seriously, lets do something!"

"Verone, this is why I love this kid," exclaimed Marona.

"Arrun, always so quick to pull the trigger. I heard you've been practicing your shot, are you already so anxious to test your skills? Young blood let me tell you something; I didn't get to the top by rushing every decision I made. Of course I want to get rid of Shekhar Khan, he's been bugging me for years. Plus he hadn't only attempted a hit on me; he tried to take my sons life as well. There is no forgiving that, and so we've waited; I guess you're right. It is time for our move isn't it? I've got a plan in store, and he won't see it coming. Be patient with me, we'll go over the plan sometime today. Though the main focus of the day is to celebrate, because it's Verone's birthday."

"Happy birthday brother," I wished Verone. I guess Marona was right; he is the wise one. I have been a bit anxious to get myself involved in the business, and it could be because I want to make a statement, but I was just tired of losing, even when all others saw recent events as a victory. With every passing moment, I could not help but think that I was going to lose another life around me.

~

The time was 6pm when I stepped into the shower, and fifteen minutes later I started hearing a call of my name. I jumped into my sweatpants and made my way down the stairs. Half way down I asked Remone to tell me who's asking for me "You have to see this for yourself," said Remone. "Aren't you going to ask me to come in," inquired a voice. It was Nilani, why on Earth did she come here? This is the last thing I needed; I actually thought I would never have to see her again.

"Not bad," she joked, as I placed my hands over my chest feeling naked.

"What the hell are you doing here?" I questioned.

"What? I can't visit a friend," she replied.

"A friend? Are you serious? How'd you get our address?" I asked.

"I'm the police commissioners daughter, remember," she answered in amusement.

"Good luck with this brother," laughed Remone as he walked out the front door.

Why me? Why me, is all I could ask myself. With everything happening around us, the last thing I needed was Nilani's attention. "Why did you come here," I asked walking back up the stairs. "I just felt like seeing you," she responded, as she followed me up, and through the door to my room. I couldn't help but think that she was catching feelings for me. What else is a guy to assume when a girl that he kidnapped came looking for him, without the police?

"Are you looking for a shirt," she asked curiously.

"No, I'm just casually digging through my clothes," I replied sarcastically.

She must have noticed my irritation to her presence, but she didn't seem to care. She was a beautiful girl and all, and sure if my mind were in the right place, I would have probably made a move by now. Unfortunately I knew mentally I would not be ready to allow another women into my life. The life I chose was not of any help either; I could lose my life at any moment these days. I would be a moron to let Nilani get close, leaving her to deal with my loss.

"You should really leave Nilani," I suggested.

"But why, couldn't we just talk for a bit," she countered.

My will was not strong enough to ask her to leave twice. A part of me wanted to talk to her from the moment I laid eyes on her. But isn't it wrong? It has only been a few months since Hasini passed, it wouldn't be right to move on so soon. Though Hasini would want me to; she wouldn't want me to be the emotional wreck that I am today. I asked God to show me a sign, could Nilani be so?

"For a bit, but not too long," I replied, giving in to her pressure.

"To be honest, I really wanted to hear you finish off your story. You know, the one that you were telling me of, on the balcony. I couldn't sleep last night, I kept thinking about you. I know how it sounds, but hear me out. I just couldn't understand why you went out of your way to

help me, and then the way you handled the situation with my father. You don't seem to be like the rest of them; obviously there's more to you, and I just want to know. Actually, I need to know."

"First of all, I've already explained why I saved you. I have or had many important women figures in my life, and I wouldn't have let anything happen to them. If you're referring to me taking you home, instead of keeping you captive, there's reasoning for that too. I used you as my bargaining chip to get your dad off our case; he was working with another criminal to kill my boss. Who by the way is actually more of father figure to me now, something I grew up without."

"Why the hostility? I know you're just trying to push me away. I just don't get why."

"Do you really want to know, because I'm actually tired of keeping everything a secret from everyone. People are always so lost, wondering why I do things the way I do. Where did I stop my story? My Siblings? I have five siblings back in Toronto, and a stepmother who passed. Life was hard but we moved on, and then I met a girl. One girl, and every aspect of my life came tumbling down. Hasini, she was the first girl I met that made me feel complete. I was going to marry her; I even bought a place for us. Unfortunately I lost her in a car accident a few months back, and it condemned me to darkness. I came here after a series of unforeseen events, and as odd as it may seem, the new life here has been helping me free my mind."

"Sorry, I didn't see that coming," she responded regretfully.

"It's alright, I wouldn't expect anyone to," I replied; walking towards my pack of smokes I asked her to join me outside. Nilani didn't utter a word as she followed me to the rooftop. She watched as I took seat at the edge of the house, looking out at the city. "Well aren't you going to join me," I asked, staring at her as she stood quietly. She smiled gracefully, prior to taking a seat next to me. "So you'll never love a girl the same," she questioned hesitantly.

"Nilani, I'll never love any else the way I did Hasini. Although there is no saying that I may love someone more, someday. I've yet to meet someone more open-minded than her; she thought of things in the most beautiful ways. With her I believed I could've lived life to full extents. There was this one time, she told me to find love even if she passes. How many girls would desire the same? The depression I've gained over the past months is not just a result of her death. I placed myself into a dark world to further understand the beliefs she passed on to me."

"She is something else, I get why you miss her so much," replied Nilani. We remained quiet for a brief moment before she delivered me with a shock. "Do you think it would ever work between us?" she asked. I didn't know what to say, she caught me by surprise. I had a suspicion that things were going in this direction, but I didn't think it'd come so soon.

"Nilani, think before you speak. I'm a criminal Nilani; I've killed people. You're the daughter of the Police Commissioner. What makes you think that it'll ever work? You're well educated, and you've got a lot going for you in the future. Me, I walk out of the house prepared to die with every passing moment. Just walk away now Nilani; it's the best thing to do."

"Couldn't you just give it a chance Arrun," she pleaded, as a tear stroked down her cheek. I didn't know what to say; my thoughts made me believe that if she were here any longer, I maybe give the relationship a chance. "Nilani, I think its better if you leave now," I suggested, hoping she'd leave. "Fine I'll leave, but you'll love me someday, I know it!" she shouted. She got up and walked away, wiping her tears, as she took final glance at me before heading down the stairs.

I listened as I heard Nilani storm out the door, I assume she came here in hopes of things going much smoother. Staring out at the city retiring for the day, I began to question if she was in love? More over was I in love? No, it can't be possible. I hardly even know her, how am I to call this love? Then again, why did I care so much? She was a just another person, nothing but a job. That is all I did right, my job? It was the first glance wasn't it; she whirled me in. So easily, am I really that vulnerable? Wait, what if it was the similarities; Nilani reminded me of Hasini a numerous amount of times. Is it wrong for me to run into her arms because she reminded me of Hasini? She wouldn't want to be Hasini; how can a girl like being compared to another?

Forget me caring so much, how will I explain this to Marona and the others. They won't be pleased to know that I have been getting close to the Commissioners daughter. I can't allow my personal life to collide with business; it will never work. She's going to get hurt, and people are going to meet ends if this goes any further. It was right for me to let her go.

My battling state of mind was interrupted by a phone call from Remone; he wanted to be picked up on my way to the Duranji residence. It took me a few minutes to get ready and head out, but Remone waited at a nearby street side coffee shop. I guess we had some time for a coffee;

we shared a cigarette while sipping down some coffee.

"Arrun, look over there," exclaimed Remone, as he pointed in the direction of some stranger. "I didn't know you were into guys bro! Sorry, I have no expertise in this department, but you got my support," I responded amusingly. "That's Khans only son Abdul, you idiot," replied Remone; it was obvious he didn't know what to do. I guess the stranger wasn't much of stranger after all.

> *"Alright Remone, listen close cause this is what you'll have to do. Take the jeep, and wait for my signal. When I give you the signal, drive towards us as I take out the man next to him, and then toss Khans son into the car."*

If we can get a hold of Khans son, we'll be able to set some fear in Khan. Opportunity came and decided to have a coffee across the street from us; we would be fools to turn it down. I walked a bit down the street before crossing sides; the two of them remained calm as I drifted in the back unnoticed. Standing two meters apart from them both, I signaled Remone to drive by. The next few actions must be quick; pulling out my pistol I didn't think twice before firing the first shot, it drove right through the head of Abdul Khan's companion. My hands were too deep in cold water to care of adding another person to my list of kills; remaining calm I pistol whipped Abdul leaving him to fall unconscious. After throwing him in the jeep we drove off, watching the pedestrians stare at us in fear along the street of the local stores. It did not feel great knowing that I had become a monster; nevertheless I knew that my emotions needed to be slain.

The time was around 9:45pm, I asked Remone to drop me off at the Duranji residence before taking Abdul Khan to a safe house. I have already been receiving phone calls from Raja and Verone for being late. As soon as it maybe, even Miran gave me a call to reach the party as soon as possible. The drive wasn't too long; Remone dropped me off at the front gate as he drove off quick. We did not want to cause a commotion, just in case the guests noticed the unconscious body of Abdul lying in the back of the vehicle.

I knew I was late when I walked through the towering front gates; the decorations were at its finest surrounding the magnificent work of architecture the Duranji's called home. The finest vehicles of the guests were lined up in the driveway; I haven't even met anyone yet, but I knew that there were bundles of important people in my presence. I worked my way through the driveway, shaking the hands of fellow henchmen before stepping through the front door. There sat Marona, like a king as usual, in his abnormally large sized chair.

"Arrun! Come here! I want you to meet some people," he called out.

I didn't really care about meeting any one of them, but I put on my signature fake smile as I sat around a group of politicians, corporate gurus, high-ranking police officers, local thugs, along with Verone, Raja, and Miran. I was in, if it was not clear to me before, it is now. Introductions, and casual conversations over a few drinks continued to be the theme over the next hour before a time of separation. Interrupting the conversation, Marona got up as everyone went quiet. "Excuse us. Arrun, Miran, Verone, Raja, could I speak to you guys for a brief moment," asked Marona.

We all got up, and I noticed that Miran was having some difficulty getting up. He was still wearing the brace from earlier that day, so I offered to help. "Thank you brother," he said as I put his arm around my shoulder. After taking seat in the nearby room, Marona began to run through the plan to control Shekhar Khan.

"Arrun you were right earlier today when you said we've been taking the hit for far too long. Which is why I've come up with a plan; how do you like the sounds of taking out all of Khan's front-runners, leading to the kidnapping of his only son. That should really shake him up. We'll separate into groups, and have certain members deal with their respective targets. Arrun I want you running the point on kidnapping Abdul Khan."

"Done, did the job two hours ago with Remone," I said calmly as I stared at the floor. The room remained haunted of shock for a while before Verone got out of his chair. He came crouched down before me, looked me in the eye and asked, "Are you serious right now?" I didn't speak a word before Verone asked me to get up. "You're the man brother, holy fuck," he exclaimed as he hugged me in major excitement. I took a look at the three other personals in the room and you could tell that they were astonished.

"Where is he," questioned Raja eagerly.

"I don't know yet, Remone is hiding him somewhere safe," I replied.

"Find out! We need to know," he continued.

"Raja let it be. Arrun is running the point on this remember," interrupted Marona.

"Well, what are we waiting for? Lets celebrate," shouted Verone as he dragged me out the room. As we walked out, Remone made his way through the front door. Verone tugged me towards Remone; he placed his arms around the both of us. The backyard of the house was decorated even grander than the front. With beautiful women, booze, and friends to company. Verone, Remone, and I took a numerous amount of shots before we separated. It has been a while since I have had this many drinks, so long that I forget how much fun I used to have drinking at parties.

Remone and I continued to sip down alcohol as Verone separated from us. Soon after an intoxicated Thambi came bulldozing his way towards us, bringing more alcohol, as if we had not had enough. As we drank that down, Renny and Sethu came rushing towards us, wasted, with more alcohol. As they held the booze in their hands I could only wonder; hey, why not right? By the end of that, we were surely wasted. To be honest it felt great, I felt loose. It felt amazing having drink with people in a positive mindset. Much greater than drinking to the negative thoughts I had a few weeks back.

It didn't take long before we began to notice the amount of gorgeous women we were surrounded by. Renny started hollering at them to get their attention, and attention is what we got.

"Well are you guys just going to stand there, or dance with us," questioned a beauty amongst the crowd of many. A look to my left, Thambi and Remone smiled. A look to my right, Renny and Sethu smiled. "Oh God!" I screamed as we dropped our beers at a synchronized rate, and rushed our way towards them. We danced amongst them all; I finally remembered what it felt like to actually enjoy something.

A memorable night it was, as we eventually got Verone, Miran, Raja, many other henchmen, and even Marona to dance with us. I started to get a real sense of family around this group of guys. I actually enjoyed the night enough to lose focus of the time passing by. Before we knew it, the time neared 3am; the guests began to head home as I sat at the steps of the front door with my four roommates, accompanied by a few other guys. We sipped chilled down imported Heineken beer, my favorite; it reminded me of home.

It was nearly a half hour passed 3am when most had left home. However suddenly there was this one car with bright headlights pulling into the driveway. Everyone became alerted, especially because the vehicle seemed unfamiliar. The door opened, and Nilani stepped out, she looked furious. Everyone remained on red-alert, as they recognized her as the Police Commissioners daughter. "Cool down, Cool down. She's just a girl," I said amusingly as she continued to brisk towards me. BAM! I nice tight slap to my right cheek, I could swear the world shook for a brief moment; I didn't see it coming.

"That's for keeping me up at night, with thoughts of you," she yelled.

I stood steady and speechless as she took a step closer. She stood right at my neck, as she glanced up towards me. She exhaled heavily and then she kissed me, I didn't want to pull back, I could not pull back. Instead I placed my left arm around her waist, embracing her closer. With my right hand I graced her hair over her ear, and kissed her back. Cheering and chanting roared in the back, as I felt completely drifted to another world. All my nerves sent signals to my mind, producing millions of thoughts; scrambled, as it created enhanced feelings that had to be deciphered. The moment felt so long, but surprisingly, I didn't mind. She slowly moved back, as my hands let go of her. Falling to reality, I heard the boys screaming in the back. I was completely intoxicated, but it definitely was not the alcohol. In fact, the alcohol seemed to have vanished completely from my body. Instead, I was intoxicated to a long lost feeling I once experienced before. Her face glowed of something similar, she walked backwards as she bit her lips. With a final smile she got in her car and reversed out; and I dropped.

Thambi caught me in the motion and lifted me back up, and when I turned around I felt like some celebrity. Everyone was hyping me, pushing me around, as I remained astonished. Looking further out, I saw Verone clapping, and of more importance, Marona with a giant smile across his face; it didn't suit him at all, but it was good to see him smile.

What a day.

Part 3: So It Begins

Chapter 13 – To Fall In and Out of Love

The morning arrived, and drenched within my blankets I could not help but think of Nilani. It was different, usually I would be contemplating whether I could think of someone else after Hasini passed, but in this instant that wasn't the cause for my struggle of thoughts. Instead the choice was totally up to me; there really was nothing holding me back. From the moment I set eyes on her, I felt something. I have been trying to push back feelings, but that could only be done for a limited period, before it overpowers my mentality completely.

I twisted and turned, stuffed my face in my pillow and screamed. In the world around me, I have become somewhat of a criminal icon. Yet, in my room I remain a love-struck soul. Remone knocked on my door before popping his head through.

"Bro, is everything alright in here," he asked.

"Yeah." I replied, hoping he wouldn't make an annoying joke.

"Good, cause you've got a guest," he said as he opened the door wider. Nilani; I sat up on my bed, using blankets to cover my boxer wearing lower half.

"I'll leave you both to it, behave kids," joked Remone.

"Get the fuck out bro," I shouted, throwing a pillow at the door.

Nilani closed the door behind her as she came and sat at the corner of my bed. I actually felt nervous, I didn't know how to start the conversation as I watched her sit quietly. I should probably say something though. "I'm sorry for slapping you," she spoke; just as I was about instigate conversation. "Don't worry, I haven't even thought about it," I replied. We returned to our awkward silence, neither one of us had a clue of how to start the more important conversation. It would probably sound better if I speak up first.

"The both of us can't just sit here the rest of the day. So, I might as well throw it out there. Obviously there was something different about the moment we shared last night. I mean."

"Sorry Arrun, could I say something first? I was the one to fall for you first; I'm the one who has been drenched in a whole bunch of thoughts over the past few days. I'd rather speak it all now, and it won't be long, so just listen. I get why you can't be with me, it's partially because of the

things you're involved with here. Though we both know the real reason. You still love Hasini, and there probably is no replacing her, but maybe it's okay to fall in and out of love? I mean, I know I may never replace Hasini in your heart, and I can't make you either. What if I could try to love you as much as she did? I can see through your dark cover, I know you have the heart to love a lot. Maybe you can give me a small portion of that love? Maybe someday I can be what Hasini was for you. I know it's a bunch of what ifs and all, but that's how things happen right? We won't know unless we give it a shot."

"You're right, it's a bunch of maybes and what ifs, but I'll never know unless I give it a shot. It's hard to explain the thoughts that crossed my mind when we kissed last night. Everything around me just went blank; I forgot about my past, I forgot about everything that has happened here but you. You were the only thought on my mind; it was all you, multiplied a thousand times over and over again. I never thought for a second that I'd find someone who can make me feel that way again, but you did. You make me feel like it's possible to love more than once, maybe love more than the first time itself. I've recently felt like all cross roads in my life brought me here to live this chaotic lifestyle; now I think otherwise. Maybe I climbed mountains for you; I've never been a firm believer in fate, but it could actually exist. I don't know how things will go for me from here on out, but one thing is certain. I want you in my life."

I didn't even finish before she jumped on top of me, holding me tight. I couldn't breath, but I was fine with it. She slept at my side for a few minutes before she began asking me to go out with her.

"My wallet isn't going to be a happy one in this relationship, is it?" I asked.

"Hell no," she replied, laughing beautifully with the morning sun gracing her skin through the windows. I don't know if Hasini was still present around me, but I know for a fact that she will be glad that I met someone like Nilani.

"Now stop being half-naked and get ready, I'll wait downstairs," she commanded, walking out the door to my room. It didn't take too long to get ready, but on my way out the door I did something strange. I looked at myself in the mirror, something I haven't done in awhile. I noticed that I smiled all while I got ready, a sense of light in my dark cave.

The time was around 8am when I came down, and my four roommates were already up and about. It was quite funny seeing Nilani at the table eating breakfast with them. She fit in well, and that was surely a plus point. "She's a keeper bro," said Remone, as I shifted my attention to Sethu. I remember how Sethu felt about the incident at the brothel. He was upset, that I attacked Miran to defend Nilani; I waited hoping for him to say something. "I was wrong about her brother, glad you're happy," he voiced; a little weird and quiet, but he surely did care for his friends.

Nilani had already ate breakfast with my friends, so instead of going out to grab a bite, she drove us over to a nearby beach. Marina Beach; apparently it is really famous in Chennai. Many scattered along the beach, it was actually quite surprising considering the fact that it was so early in the morning. Couples, families, and concession stands were scattered all around. It was pretty hard to find a place to sit at first, but we eventually did. Nilani was over at a concession stand, grabbing us two cups of tea. I sat there staring out into the waters, wondering of how much my life will change with the presence of Nilani. My lifestyle is meant for me to care about no ones life, but I actually have someone to live for now.

"What are you thinking about," she asked as she took seat next to me on the warm sand beneath us. "I don't know what to do anymore," I replied, continuously beating my mind of the future.

"Life changes a lot from here," I stated.

"Not really, I'm not going to ask you to change everything for me, you know what's best for you. You're smart Arrun, you don't need to live the life of a criminal. You can go about and find a great job and still lead an incredible life, and it's totally in your hands. It may be hard, starting from the bottom, but I'll be here through the struggle."

"I can't just walk away Nilani, I'm pretty far into this mess. I'm surrounded by devils, not to mention that I'm no saint myself. I don't support half the things the people around me do. Corrupt politicians, crooked officers, all bowing down to the criminal world. It's hard to watch the lives of innocent people collapse, all because of actions of people with higher authority. Things have to change, but some people must go for those issues to be fixed. I'm drowning in issues around me, and I can't think of change until those problems are dealt with. It does feel great though, knowing that you'll be at my side through it all."

"How will your dad react to us," I questioned curiously, he is not going to be ecstatic that his daughter is with an unlawful person like me.

"He wants to speak with you, he's observed me being unusual," she said.

"What do you mean?" I asked.

"He noticed something different about me. It started the day you left me at the front gate of my house. He feels that there is more to you than an ordinary criminal."

"To be honest, I don't think this is the life I want to lead forever. Your presence made me realize this, but I can't let go of the impact my position can have. My voice is actually respected amongst the group of criminals I'm surrounded by. I can actually spark a change, but it'll have to come after we deal with a few issues."

From the moment I saw that elderly driver killed in the street shootout, I could not help but notice that amount of lives being impacted by our actions. Then there were the women in the brothel; some there because there is no other way to support their families, but I wouldn't be surprised if they are forcefully there. It isn't right, and after the Khan issue is over I must talk to Marona about change.

"Wait, we've been talking so much about me. Tell me some stuff about you," I asked.

"Uhm my life isn't quite as exciting as yours, so I'll keep it short. I plan parties for a living, I know, its like, is that even a job? But yeah, I love it. Especially when you see the amount of people who come out and enjoy. I work with my friend/business partner Dipti, she's not Tamil like the both of us. She's Punjabi, and boy is she a blast to be around. Pretty sure you're dying to know of my past boyfriends, there were only two, and they were both idiots. My mom passed away when I was a kid, never really got to know her. I've always been spoiled by my dad, he's awesome, trust me! Beyond the tough police officer front he puts up, he's really soft and cute! Oh there's another thing you can probably relate to. You know Shekhar Khans son Abdul? Yeah that guy is such a pig! He annoys me so much; I think my dad must have mentioned me once. Ever since then, he's been trying to hit on me, like nonstop! He's such a pervert; I wish he'd just be washed off the face of the planet."

If only she knew that we had him locked up and beaten down right now. As amusing as it was, I couldn't let her know. I wouldn't want her to get hurt, especially if it is because of my actions.

I wanted to continue talking with her throughout the day, but I got a phone call from Remone saying the operation had started. It was going to be a busy day, and I had to head home now.

Nilani dropped me off at my place, where I saw Remone, Sethu, Thambi, and Renny ready to go. She waived goodbye, and Remone checked to see if I was a go for today. I knew I had to keep one life away from another. "Let's get on with it brother," I said, as we all got in one vehicle.

Chapter 14 – Boils Over

"Where'd you keep him," I asked, as Remone drove. "One of our factories, it's only five minutes away," he responded. As we drove silent and anxiously, I knew that today would be the day it all boils over. The on going issues between the two groups can come to an end today, or it could just get bad, real quick. Either way, this needed to end. Too many lives have been lost, or have been affected over the power struggle. I would rather have this issue come to an end now; I'm not willing to lose anyone else.

As Remone pulled in, the three story high factory seemed deserted of sorts. There were still a few vehicles upfront, but they were probably that of our men. It was quite isolated from the city, and so I highly doubt anyone would come to know of the location unless told. Moreover, the place just looked creepy, like it was meant for bad deeds. "You sure know how to pick locations Remone," I said as the others laughed. "I know this place looks beautiful, kind of like paradise," added Sethu. We all turned our attention to him and simply nodded our heads, side to side. It's when he says things like that; you can't help but wonder the sick, twisted things that go on in his head.

Shaking off Sethu's weird comment, we made way inside where a few henchmen were keeping things under control. "We'll take over here now, why don't you help with the other operations," I suggested, as they agreed. After they left I sat around with my four friends, going over the game plan.

"We got hold of Abdul last evening, so the search for him has probably been underway for a while now. On our side, I say we wait it out. We should wait to receive calls from our men, till after they make the hit on all of Khans guys. After we receive confirmation I'll make a call to Khan, how much do you think the ransom should be? How about ten million, in US dollars? That should be a plentiful, I'm pretty sure Marona would be glad to get some compensation out of all of this."

"You think he would just walk in here and just hand us the money," asked Renny.

"He would, Abdul is his only son," replied Remone.

"Exactly! Abdul is his only son, I'm pretty damn sure that he wouldn't risk losing his only son, for some cash. The guys loaded, he wouldn't care to spend a few millions, if it meant saving his son. Now Renny you're right about one aspect though, he probably will have a back up plan. Something along the lines of killing the five of us, saving his son, and keeping his money, but we aren't going to let that happen. Once we get the call from our guys, confirming that they've whipped the targets;

we'll get them here to secure the perimeter. Making it difficult for Khan and his men to infiltrate us. Plus, they'll be short in their body count after we take out their lead men."

"Sounds good Arrun," supported Sethu.

"I'm all in, with that kind of money I wouldn't have to pay to hangout with girls," added Thambi; we had a brief moment of silence before we laughed uncontrollably. The laughs were fun, and you can always depend on Thambi to deliver, but we had to get down to business.

~

Over the course of the last six hours we been receiving calls from all our men, confirming that they have finished they're respective task. With the time closing in around 6pm, I thought this would be the right time to make the call to Shekhar Khan. Remone read out the number to me as I smiled and thought that it's quite amusing of how easy it is to get the number of an enemy, but to get the number of a beautiful girl we must go to ultimate extents. As the rings continued I waited for a response from the other side. "Hello," answered a voice. "Is Khan there," I queried.

"This is him, who is this," he confirmed.

"This is Arrun speaking; one of your dear friend Marona's men. Listen close, cause I'm not repeating myself twice. We've got your son, and so

you've got two options. You could either let him stay here, and we'll kill him within the next hour, or you can pack up $10 million dollars in cash and come meet us in exchange for your son. I'll text you the address, and you know it's probably better if you don't get the police or higher authority involved in this. You know it'll never work in your favor. You've got one hour, so act quick."

"I'm coming, I'm coming! Don't do anything to him," he pleaded.

It's easy for any person to front like they're the boss, but when put in a situation to pick family over power; things change drastically. I'm sure Khan will be storming in soon, for sure before his one hour of time is up.

I stood seated on a chair with one leg up, and as I waited for the Khans arrival Remone asked me to check on Abdul. I've yet to see the guy since we've arrived, it might be of some help to set some fear in him as well. It's one thing to tame his father, it's better to seat fear in his young blood before it gets out of hand.

He was practically imprisoned by us the past day, a dark room with a small whole of light. It was cruel, but he wasn't someone that deserved more. He was fed, what more can he ask of an enemy? As I opened the latch to the door, it was quite visible that he was getting tired of confinement. "How long are you going to fucking keep me here, I'm hungry you bitch, I need to go out" shouted Abdul. "Well that's up to your pops my friend," I replied, keeping calm; I was sure that this conversation could get bad, real quick.

"You think I don't know who you are? You're that fool from Toronto, trust me leave. You don't know the world you've entered, there is no getting out when you're too far in. Just hand me over to my father, and try walking away as fast as you can. Go back to your princess life back in the western world, while I stay here with Nilani. Your little romance with her is no secret. Know one thing for sure, once you're gone, I'll marry her. Not out of love though, I may even beat her from time to time if she fails to listen. How could we forget the fact that I'll show her what a real man could do throughout the nights; unlike little bitches that hit people from behind!"

"Abdul man, you should've just kept quiet and ate your food. Now you're going to have to continue to starve, plus the food was actually good! As for Nilani, look at you, think of her, and now look at me. Does my face look like I give a single fuck about you?"

Oh the urge, the urge to just plumage his face ran through my body the entire time. I really didn't feel the need to talk to him though; there was nothing to fear. I guess I tried to talk to him calmly and at this point his fathers fear can probably transfer over to Abdul if it hadn't already settled in.

"The guys a prick, its hard to teach these fools a lesson sometimes," I said, as Renny approached me. As he stood next to Sethu he replied," Oh brother, you just figured that out." I guess I've always been one to think that people deserve another chance, and so I had hope. Though there's always a thing about hope, it's not for everyone. "We've got word, that Shekhar Khan is almost here. With four vehicles worth of support," informed Remone. It's about time we prepare, to insure things don't go south. I prepped some of the henchmen for activity outside the factory; it was important for them to stay undetected. With the amount of men we had with us, there was no chance for us to be out numbered on the inside.

As the time neared 6:50pm we heard the amount of roaring engines pulling in. Storming in was Shekhar Khan with nearly twenty-five henchmen. They came in with guns ready to fire, but I guess he really underestimated the amount of men we'd have with us. It was quite easy to circle them all, they were forced to drop their weapons. Standing amongst the mist our man, I watched; it was easy to spot the fear in Khan's eyes. With both his hands slowly gracing the air he called out to me.

"Arrun! Which one of you is Arrun? I have the money, just let my son go!" He shouted.

My men moved out the way, as I became the centerpiece. "Couldn't you just have done this from the get go," I questioned, while the men around me held position to insure there weren't any sneak attacks. "Please, just give me back my son," he begged. I turned back to Thambi, who was standing in the back holding a tight grip of Abdul. Thambi brought him forward, as Abdul stood next to me. "Thambi, go get the bag and check it," I commanded as everyone waited for the confirmation. Its no fun playing with criminals, they can never be trusted; it'll always be plain mind games.

Once I got the nod, I gave a gentle push on his back telling him to walk slowly. He took a step forward, before turning back towards me and giving me the finger.

"Man, you really should've just kept walking," I responded; irritated to the bone.

His face woke up; noticing the gap between both his legs, I used my left foot to kick him behind his right knee. As he dropped on both knees, I simultaneously kneeled down.

"Eye to eye, is this man enough for you?" I asked. I removed the holstered handgun behind me, pulled back the slide aiming straight between his eyes, and with no room to spare I pulled the trigger. Seconds later a loud cry is all we heard, as Shekhar Khan was forced into to tears. His men stood in shock, unable to react in anyway; weapon less, powerless.

My men waited for my command. This wasn't over just yet, as I raised my left fist in the air, the deafening roar of bullets bashing skulls of our enemies proved to be evidence to our strength. Standing strong, I looked down as the blood of Abdul streamed through the floor. Meters away, Shekhar Khans eyes remained opened wide, lost and alone.

It was scary, my heart didn't race, and things seemed to be perfectly fine. Instead, I was able to hear the increasing pulse of Khans heart, with every step I took towards him. Speechless he remained, glaring at the body of his soulless son in the distance. He couldn't even bear to look back at the dead bodies of his men around him; I holstered my gun behind me as Remone recommended that we move out.

"One second," I responded.

"Khan, look at me," I directed, as he remained blank. "When I say look at me, look at me," I ordered; he did as instructed. He stared back at me with his eyes moist in tears, crammed with fright.

"You did this, you're responsible for this. I didn't kill your son, you did. Your actions, and greed to control killed him. The only reason we're letting you walk away alive is so that you can live every second of your miserable life feeling responsible. What's better for you now is to walk away, from everything completely, and never to turn back. This is our place; don't try to take our place. Things are going to change; you're the example we're setting. Step down!"

On that note we walked, leaving behind what is now a man with an ample amount of regrets; it's really hard to suffer anything more. At his age, killing him would've been a blessing.

~

I came out a criminal hero of sorts; I could see it through the way most of the guys reacted once we returned to the Duranji residence. I guess my actions have a tendency to be extremely anarchist, but I like to think that my actions are usually for the greater good. Criminals surround me; obviously they loved what I did today. I thought I did too, but on our ride over I tried thinking it over, and it may have been horrible decision making on my part. I may have let my anger get the best of me, and I'm pretty sure that's what Remone thought. I noticed that he remained quiet while we drove here; all while Thambi, Sethu, and Renny continuously praised my method of handling situations.

I could see the same look in Verone's face; it's probably why the both of them are so close, they think alike. Marona is usually the first one up congratulating me, but today, even he seemed to be fairly quiet. I knew I was becoming a monster when it was Miran who came up to hug me. "You're the man," he preached; I didn't know whether I should be glad that we're getting along or upset about it. The fact that we were getting along was good for the business and family, but it meant I was becoming more like him, that's not what I wanted, especially cause I initially hated his guts.

"Lets get some drinks going tonight," recommended Miran, and so that's exactly what we did. The time was around 11pm when we began popping bottles left and right; we were on a tear. An hour later I was beyond wasted; some of the guys continued to talk about the way I shot Abdul. Remone remained quiet; he hardly even drank. Then there was Thambi who sat next to Remone, drinking shot after shot, beer after beer, all while stuffing huge pieces of chicken down his throat. "Thambi you got to chill, you're going to choke brother," I teased. "I'm still hungry though," he replied; he wasn't even joking.

Soon it was around 1am, when everyone was beginning to lose it. Some of the guys were way out of it. Sethu, and Renny were literally sleeping on top of each other. Remone stepped away with Thambi to smoke a joint, leaving Miran and I to have a quiet conversation.

"Hey Arrun, what does it feel like to be in love?" Asked Miran.

"Oh man, you really are wasted. You do realize that a question about love doesn't even suit your face," I clowned.

"Quit joking around man, I'm actually serious," he replied.

"Well then, I did not expect this from you! I really don't know what to tell you bro, it's easier to fall in love than to actually explain it. Love is actually a false term; we are not whole without the people in our lives. You meet some great people, who partially add up to try and fill the whole piece, and I guess the person that you fall in love with is the one that completes most of that whole? I don't know brother, I'm wasted!"

"Believe it or not, that actually makes sense. So is that the way you feel about Nilani?" He asked.

"Oh for sure, to be honest with you I feel like I've changed so much since I've gotten here. I feel like she keeps me sane, and it maybe too soon to say, but I think I want to spend the rest of my life with her. I've fallen in "love" before, but there is something about Nilani that makes me feel like she completes me a lot more than I expected, a lot more than I need her too."

"Oh god! What a line, what a line," teased Miran.

"Shut the fuck up," I replied. I knew he was just messing around, that dude and love would forever remain at a distance. When Remone returned I knew he was pretty high, he actually began speaking to me again. "This guy is my best friend," I shouted; unable to control his laughter he responded, "Bro, you are so smashed."

"Smashed or not, I still love you brotha!" I shouted.

Like that, things went into a momentary blur. Minutes later, I felt like we magically ended up near Nilani's house. "Get out Arrun," said Remone.

"Why on earth did you bring me here," I asked; I was totally confused.

"Are you serious right now? You fucking begged and annoyed the shit out of me to drive you here. You're getting out!" Shouted Remone.

"I did, didn't I?" I responded, as bits and pieces of a conversation came to mind.

"Yeah you retard! Now get out, Thambi is sleeping. I don't want to risk him waking up, he's going to end up asking me to buy him a "snack", and we both know how much that ends up being."

"Thambi!" I shouted, waking him up. Remone was right on, Thambi wanted to buy more food. Like that, Remone was upset with me again, but it was hilarious. Though the joke was on me, because I was the one stuck outside the gated house. I didn't even know which side of the house Nilani's room was on, but I knew this wasn't going to be as easy as walking through the front door past the security of a Police Commissioners house.

I walked around the concrete wall built to fence the house, and noticed that there was a balcony on the back end. Hopping the wall was a piece of cake; I did it with much ease, my athleticism definitely helped. It seemed easier to sneak through the yard of an officer than expected, well until I saw the sleeping guard dog. That's when I had thoughts of becoming a track star, but maybe I should attempt to walk by as quickly and quietly as possible. It took me nearly half an hour to walk past the guard dog undetected, I could have done it faster, but my sober state of mind has taken a hit for sure!

I probably shouldn't have bragged about how easy it was to sneak in, cause things seemed to be getting more difficult by the second. The bottom doors were locked, obviously. I should've knocked myself in the head for even considering it to be open; my only option would be to climb the extremely narrow pole up to the balcony.

Man oh man, that wasn't easy at all. My first two attempts were a total fail, and the third attempt would've been horrible if I didn't grasp hold of the balcony with my leap of faith. Luckily for me, the balcony doors were open! I wasn't a complete idiot; then again, here comes the hardest part. I'm in this huge house, and I have no clue of where my girlfriend's room is. Calling her was probably my best option.

"Nilani! I'm in your house," I said.

"Arrun? What time is it...wait what? You're kidding right!" She replied.

"No, I'm hiding behind your couch right now, I came through the balcony door," I responded.

"Are you stupid? What if my dad sees you? You could've just called from outside the house!" She shouted.

"Oh right, that probably would've been smarter," I said.

"Uh, you think so? I'm coming, stay quiet"

"Nilani," I whispered, in a cheerful tone. "Are you drunk," she asked. I just gave her a blank glare, watching her as she smacked her hand on her forehead. "Darling, why are you hurting yourself," I asked. Her face definitely showed frustration, she directed me to follow her quietly. I felt like one of those comedic detectives I grew up watching on TV as a kid, one finger over my lips, tippy toeing over to her room.

"Wow you are a totally different personality when drunk," she commented. I actually was, and it has been pretty evident over the years. Alcohol has helped me have a better sense of humor, though I guess I tend to be a little bit childish; I've got to maintain my youth somehow right? The alternate personality was on full loose tonight.

"Nilani lets go back to that beach!" I suggested.

"Right now? It's kind of late don't you think?" Asked Nilani.

"Not really, lets go! I left too soon earlier today," I replied.

"You're actually serious, okay let me get ready," said Nilani, walking over to her dresser.

"Alright I'll just sit over here then," I suggested, taking seat on her bed. I bounced up and down for a bit as she just gave me this look. I assume she couldn't tell if I was being serious. "Get the hell out of here," she replied, shoving me into the bathroom. Missed opportunities, oh well, it was worth a shot right? She didn't take long before she got ready, and we were back to sneaking out just minutes after my struggle to get in. At least it was a lot easier this time around, we were able to walk out the door on the bottom floor.

Sneaking past the guard dog was the hardest part, once again. This time around it was worse, she actually woke up, and I was so sure that I'd be getting torn apart by a dog. "Go back to sleep baby," said Nilani, as I kept my eyes shut. I usually handle myself without fear of terrorism men, but the dog had me squealing.

"I wasn't asking you to sleep, open your eyes you little girl," she teased.

"Do you see the size of that beast," I yelled.

"Shhhh, you're going to get us caught," warned Nilani.

We managed to get off the property without making much noise, but we had to walk for quite a while before stopping an auto-rickshaw. I managed to have a discussion with the driver about his family and life all in the span of the ride there, completely ignoring Nilani's presence. She didn't seem to care though, I think she actually enjoyed the drunk me at times. She laughed at numerous points, and it was great to know that I was responsible for her smiles, even if it wasn't my sober-self doing so.

The beach was quiet, why wouldn't it be? It was 3am, most people would be asleep at home during these hours, but there wasn't much to complain about. There's something spectacular about a deserted beach. The noise pollution was at its minimum, allowing the deafened sea to speak. It must be the moon; it had to be the moon that made me love the darkness of the night feel brighter than the day. Though even the moon was out dueled by the beauty of Nilani, the moon couldn't help but shine bright and shed spotlight on her. I was the lucky one, graced by the gifts of life.

"Are you just going to stare at the moon Arrun?" Asked Nilani.

"Sorry, it's just that this reminds me of the first time I fell for Hasini." I replied.

"Wait, I shouldn't have said that." I cut off; I haven't considered it before, but she could be getting tired of my constant need to bring up Hasini.

"No, Arrun tell me! I'd actually like to hear about it," pressured Nilani.

"I know I bring up Hasini a lot when we speak, and I don't get how it hasn't gotten on your nerve yet, but I really appreciate it. Basically Hasini and I never got off to a dreamy start. Remember how we first met? You basically hated me, and that's exactly how it was with Hasini and me. She hated my guts when we first met, well until she found out that I was the brother of her best friend. There was this night prior to my sisters wedding where I sat down with family and friends for dinner, and she sat next to me. Hasini slipped me a note, asking me to meet her at the beach after dinner. That night at the beach, we learnt about each other for hours. We shared stories of our past, dreams for the future. You're the one that reminded me of that beautiful memory. The way you look under the moonlight right now is just amazing, I'm speechless."

She laughed uncontrollably, "Me? Beautiful? Don't lie now, I'll still love you." She responded.

"I thought I'd be nice, but fine don't take the compliment." I retorted; I thought I was hilarious, and she laughed once more before she found a stick on the ground. She chased me as a mother would if she found out her sixteen year old child was pregnant.

She actually landed a few hits on me before I was able to grab hold of her, dropping to the soft sand. I laid down with my arms stretched far out, and as she placed her head on my chest I wrapped my arm around her. Flat on my back, glaring at the stars, this time without the pain of a bullet, but with the satisfaction of comfort.

Having Nilani in my life is a blessing; well having a girl to love is a blessing for any man. Not just to know that you've got someone to love, but to know there is someone to talk to. As a man our biggest crisis has to be keeping thoughts drenched within us. We aren't able to speak of everything that bothers us, due to the fact that we need to present ourselves as the alpha-male. It isn't like that with Nilani, and it wasn't like that with Hasini. I believe that I could actually share everything on my mind, and they'd accept it and give me genuine feedback.

"Nilani, how are we going to lead a good life together?" I asked.

"I know you'll keep me happy Arrun, I see that in you." She replied, but I didn't know if that was possible. I had to constantly consider reality, I live the life of a criminal, and my intentions of fixing the group of people I'm around will surely take time.

> "Nilani I killed Abdul today. I didn't want to, I let the anger get the best of me. I've silently thought about it, and I think it was best for the lives of many people that he's dead. Then I considered the amount of lives I've taken, since I crossed this path. I'm in Nilani, in over my head. I can't even count the number of people, I've killed, and I've just been doing it left and right off instincts. I can't help but think of the monster I've

become. I'm part of a life that ruins the lives of people, the amount of family that are going to end up on the streets, lost dreams of children, and I don't even know what my sister and mother would think of me if they knew I was part of group of people who are responsible for capturing girls off the street. Those girls are taken away from their loved ones, have their lives ruined, all to hold a lump sum of money that will eventually perish to our greed. We live in a world that needs saving, and before blaming politicians we need to try and control people like me."

"No Arrun, not people like you." Condoled Nilani.

"Nilani! Look at me! I'm responsible for so much!" I cried, it was too much to bear; I was actually beginning to feel guilt. I started to feel responsible for parts of the negativity the world produces. "Hasini, would hate me right now! Don't you?" I asked.

"Take a second to think, you keep thinking off all the bad things you've done. You've never really considered the fact that you know what to fix. Remember what I told you, I could see through you. Behind the hard front you put up, you've got the biggest heart I've ever seen. You want to see things change, and you've got the voice to lead people to change. Stop tearing up like a little baby Arrun."

She whipped the tear from my eyes, before leaning back against my chest. I smiled; it was one of those moments. The moment you smile, and have no absolute clue as to why you have a big grin on your face. I closed to rest, hoping for a new road.

~

My eyes opened to glistening of the suns rays, it was murderous with my head throbbing. I knew I drank too much last night, and it didn't help as Nilani pounded my chest to wake up. "Arrun your phones ringing," she whispered. The number wasn't familiar, but it was probably one of the guys calling from the Duranji house.

"Hello?" I responded, in my wakening tone. A brief moment of silence woke me up.

"Hello?" I repeated.

"You did set fear in me. I stood in fear glancing down at my motionless son. You made me regret ever entering this life. I've been fighting with Marona for years now, and I've never stood shocked till I saw you shoot my son. Though when the fear faded, and that it did, only revenge boiled in my blood. I haven't even done my final rites for my son yet, not until I show you what fear is. Have you got a call from your friends? Remone, Thambi; do those names ring a bell? You think they got home after they dropped you off at the Commissioners house? Why don't you give them a call, check up on them."

"Khan, don't do it!" I shouted, before hearing the line go dead. I rushed to call both their phones, and I didn't get a response from either one of them. "Is everything okay?" Inquired Nilani; she must have seen my face light up with fear for the worst possible situation. "Nilani, go home! Text me when you're home safe!" I ordered, as I caught an auto-rickshaw for her safe passage.

I didn't want to think of the worst, but I can't underestimate the extents a man would go to after watching his only son being killed before his own eyes. Moments later the phone rang again, this time around I didn't wait a second before answering.

"Khan, Khan! Leave them alone; it's me you want, come get me! I'm at Marina Beach." I informed.

"I guess you called your friends, they didn't answer did they. I'd be surprised if the fat one did, seeing how he's been chopped piece by piece, scattered all across Chennai. The other one has been fairly quiet, since we made him watch your buddy get slashed up. I think he maybe traumatized; do you feel the fear sinking in yet? We're veterans kid, don't come to play the game if you aren't prepared for war. You may want to hurry up and make it to Napier Bridge, well that is if you want to save your friend."

Chapter 15 - Tables Turn, Bridges Burn

He was right, fear; I felt it creep down my spine. This wasn't a sadistic joke; it was reality. I quickly stopped the next rickshaw coming my way, and as I told him the destination I called Verone to inform him of the situation. I was closer to the bridge, but this situation wasn't going to go well if I were alone. I kept putting grave pressure on the driver, and he responded by driving faster. Napier Bridge was just six minutes from Marina beach, and by the time we made it there I practically jumped into the oncoming traffic. The rickshaw driver began yelling for his money, as I walked through the cars, honking, trying their best to avoid hitting me.

I stood confused and worried for a few seconds; I couldn't spot Khan or his men. I was beginning to think that this was all a big diversion, maybe a trap. Though it wasn't, they did come, and when they came it was with full force. A few vehicles, and dozens of men; they blocked the oncoming traffic. All but helpless stood a crowd of civilians, as if they were prepared to watch a show.

Khan was first to step out, and behind him was a man dragging out Remone. He was beaten and bloody, at first I couldn't even identify him. When the rest of Khans men stepped out, I knew that my only chance of saving my friend would be to hand over my head.

"Khan leave Remone! It's me you want!" I shouted.

He shrugged off my offer with a smile; the look of revenge was evident in his eyes. I wanted to hope that Thambi was still alive, but I wasn't stupid. I know Khan wasn't lying when he said Thambi's body was scattered across the city. I have the blood of a friend on my hands already; I wasn't ready to allow that of another spill over too. At this point I had one shot at saving my friend, and it maybe at the cost of offering my own head. The fear had already gotten to me, throughout my entire stint of life I never truly experienced fear until I had another persons life in my hands, the life of a person I actually cared about.

Nervous, and embodied in terror I ran towards Remone, hoping they'd let him go. A trip, summoned the cards for a change in scenario. I fell to the floor, bashing my head against the hard surfaced road, and when I glanced up I saw Remone being forced down to his knees. His face was partially covered in dry blood, as a few drips warmly drenched out. His head was down, but he looked up to take a quick glimpse at me.

"They cut up Thambi, right in front of me. Don't spare them Arrun." Cried Remone; as I watched Khans men hand him a machete. Remone knew what was coming; he dropped his head back down. I felt a bit dizzy because of the knock to my head, but I tried to will myself up.

It was too late; I felt my sanity take part. I watched as my best friends head rolled across the floor. Traumatized, my brain couldn't process what happened before my eyes. My eyes widened and I dropped to the floor once again, bashing the floor in the rage, as the tears ran down my face. It's on me, all me. I noticed a familiar feeling creeping back into my life, the questioning of my existence, and the thought of death following those around me. I could just lay on the floor, with my head faced to its side, listening to the machete being scraped against the floor as Khan walked towards me, or I could try and live to be the change. My death may spare the lives of a few, but this war would just continue. It was my mistake for sparing Khans life, and it must be my responsibility to end it.

A sudden breach within the crowd, as the civilians attempted to flee the scene, my support came thrashing in. I watched as my men pulled in, attempting to gun down the counter part. It was a shame though, they were prepared to drive off; the first of the few vehicles drove by picking up Khan, as the others provided cover. I got back on two feet attempting to catch up with the first car; "Arrun!" Called a voice from behind, it was a man in the last of Khans vehicles. It was odd because he was masked unlike the others, and I tried to grasp hold of his mask in my quick glancing second but to my loss, I received a demolishing hit from a metal rod to my chest.

I felt miserable, desperately trying to grasp breath. Sethu and Renny were the ones to help me up. "Remone, where's Remone!" I cried, still unable to come to terms of what I witnessed. They both cried, attempting to calm me down.

"Don't let Verone see the body!" I warned them, but it was too late. I knew of the bond the both of them shared. Marona attempted to console Verone as he held the headless body of a brother; I never expected to see such reactions from men who normally show no emotions at all. Miran, along with a few other men continued to race down the street, in hopes of catching up with Khan. I knew it was a long shot, it seemed as if they had already planned according to every possible situation.

"Where's Thambi Arrun?" Asked Renny.

"We have to kill them." I responded.

"Where's Thambi!" Questioned Renny once more.

"Look at Remone! You think they spared Thambi? They cut him to pieces and scattered him across the city. We can't even give him his last rites." I cried.

"Lets go, right now." Sethu cried.

It felt right; I didn't want to say no. I too felt the rage that boiled amongst my friends; Khan didn't deserve to live another day. Hot headed, ragged of revenge we tried walking over to the car.

"Stop!" Ordered Marona.

"Why, how long will we stand watching people die?" I retorted.

"Arrun, you aren't thinking straight. We'll talk about this later." Suggested Marona, I didn't want to argue with him, but I didn't want wait as another day went by. Another day, waiting for Khan to make his next plans; I killed his son; he wasn't going to be satisfied just yet.

"And what? Do you ask me to watch him kill someone else? It could be Renny, Sethu, me, maybe even you the next time!" I pressured.

"Arrun, stop! Remone deserves to be rested first," spoke Verone; I didn't feel right listening to Marona, but I felt the need to respect what Verone had to say. Remone was the first person I had ever considered a friend; and I should feel ashamed to have not considered resting my friend before acting out of spite.

~

We thought we had won, I thought we had won. I felt that I'd finally be able to walk away from a life of death. I thought I could bring change to the world, cancelling the wrongs we commit on a daily basis. Instead I stood amongst a crowd of all our men, furiously mourning the death of two brothers. One of which we weren't even able to find. Verone lit the fire, cremating the remains of Remone. I stared deep into the heavily breathing fire; replicating the colour of a murderous setting sky.

No one spoke a word, and when Verone began walking away towards the vehicle the rest of us followed. Renny took the wheel, and we remained silent on the drive back to the Duranji's. The silence was of peace; it provided time for us to process things out. I attempted to put the rage aside, trying to find smarter means of dealing with this situation. Though one thing is certain, the end shall not be peaceful.

Last night we were one as a family, celebrating what was assumed to be a victory, and now the house usually filled with life, fell silent. Most our men were scattered across the house, trying to get their mind off things. I sat on a couch across from Verone and Marona, remaining quiet as the both of them did too.

"I'm home safe, I hope everything is fine." Read a text I received from Nilani. She sent it quite early in the day, but I was in no mindset to respond.

"Arrun, can you come with me for a minute?" Requested Marona, as he led me to the room where we first planned to silence Khan. I was so sure that he had come up with a plan to make a return hit, but he surprised me.

"I'm sorry," he said.

"What? Why are you apologizing?" I asked.

"My fault, its my fault that you've become like this. I didn't realize what

I've made you become till I saw your eyes earlier today. The rage I saw was monstrous, it wasn't you kid, and I'm responsible for you becoming this way. You should go back to Toronto, walk away from this life! Take Nilani with you and be happy, you could still do it. Get married, have kids, it's all in the cards for you! I've made you a criminal, I felt like I saw myself in you. Though today I realized the amount of hate I have for myself, I can't stand aside and watch you become the person I am."

"Marona, do you hear yourself? You yourself realized that you're better than all of this! I've been meaning to talk to you about change, change for the better. We don't need to kill to make a statement. We shouldn't enlist fear in ordinary citizens, that's what were doing wrong! Criminals, Politicians, and anyone of higher authority, those are the ones we want to tame. We have power, we can use it for a better purpose, and it starts with you realizing that this isn't the life you want to die living."

"Arrun, just listen! You should go back to Toronto!" He insisted.

"But why? Don't you see my vision for change?" I replied.

"Change will not come without a war! Your father wouldn't want this!" He snapped.

"My father? What?" I asked. My thoughts began to run curiously; I don't understand why my dead father is involved in this.

"I'm sorry." He repeated, as a tear drenched down his face.

~

The year was 1985; a year after Marona had finished his ten-year sentence for a mass murder he committed when he was eighteen. Standing aside him in crime was his trusted childhood friend Durai, who had helped him commit the murder. Durai had come out of prison two years earlier, he was now married and expected to be a father quite soon.

Marona's initial cause for actions came out of revenge. With the assistance of Durai, he killed the people that were responsible for the murder of the Duranji family. Durai, didn't really have anyone but Marona to call family, and practically grew up a child of the Duranji household. They were inseparable, and they continued to be inseparable as they raised anarchy across the streets of Chennai. Over the period of a few months, they were starting to grasp attention from people all over India. They began taking out the top kingpins, leading to the association of friends with higher authority.

Time and influence are the two chemical compounds responsible for ones change in path. Such was what happened between the two; as the business collided with criminal activities, Raja was brought in to help share the load. Durai on one hand was being forced to walk away from the life by his wife, for the sake of his newborn child. Yet his loyalty remained with his friend, but he knew it would be quite difficult raising a child in this environment.

Durai started to notice things going in the wrong direction after the addition of Raja to the crew. Sure he did bring new concepts of making money, but they came at the cost of ruining lives of innocent people. At first it was just murders, murders of people who did wrong things; now its prostitution, smuggling, trafficking, and more. All at the beginning stages, give it a few years more, and who knows where this will end up.

Unlike Durai, Marona had the negative influence of Raja winding him in the wrong direction. He started to present Marona of the wealth and glory that awaits him in the future, all that won't come if Durai is still around.

Raja made it pretty clear to Marona that there could only be one king, and if it were to be him, Durai must die, with no loose ends.

There was a month left till Arrun's first birthday, and plans for a party were already in the works. It was a Wednesday morning, when Marona came for an unexpected visit.

"There's something I need to talk to you about." Said Marona.

"Give me a few minutes, I just got to change." Durai replied.

Devi, Durai's wife was in the kitchen cooking; while Durai was upstairs getting ready to go out, Marona stepped in to the kitchen.

"Will you be staying for lunch?" Asked Devi, unable to bear having a conversation Marona replied, "I'm sorry." He pulled out the pistol with an attached silencer that was held underneath his shirt, and reacted before Devi could even cry for help. With the sound of the cooking food, it was hard to even make out the minimal sound the pistol made.

Marona returned to the living room, and sat on the couch, attempting to play it cool.

"Alright, should we go?" Questioned Durai.

"Devi! I'll be back in a bit." Shouted Durai, he didn't wait for a response. Instead he walked out the front door, while his wife laid dead in the other room.

Marona continued to play it cool, and drove far out into empty lands. "I've decided to buy this land, what do you think," questioned Marona. Durai got out to have a look around, and in that instant Marona raised his handgun once more, the slide pulled back, ready to fire. Durai turned around, and there wasn't much of a change in his expression, even when he had a gun pointed straight for him, and that by his best friend too. Oddly enough, he may have seen it coming.

"Did you kill Devi and Arrun?" Inquired a worried Durai.

"Devi is dead, I spared Arrun." Responded Marona, as his trembled unwillingly.

"I forgive you brother," said Durai. Marona was left in total confusion; he couldn't understand why Durai was forgiving him. Where was the anger? Where was the immediate attempt for revenge? The more time he wasted, the more he began to doubt if he were doing the right thing, but the fear consumed him.

His shaking hands gave in, his second thoughts didn't matter, and the first bullet hit Durai straight near the heart. Marona couldn't watch as Durai struggled to hold on to his life, he pulled the trigger three more times to insure an immediate death.

~

"Your dad forgave me, I tried to killed him; its been haunting me!" Cried Marona.

I didn't know what to say; I mean the guy before my eyes killed both my parents, but I couldn't feel the rage. But then the rage I felt when Sarah passed, the anger of losing Hasini, and then losing both Remone and Thambi fuelled more anger. This just presented me with possibilities of a life I could've had.

"I swear I didn't know you were Durai's son when you first came," continued Marona, as he tried to reason for his actions. "Raja figured it out first, when the both of you first met," he added.

"Arrun, just do it. Kill me, please free me," pleaded a lost Marona; he was tired of being a monster. I could really just kill him, but I'd just lose another important piece to the puzzle, and that wasn't worth it. Yet I still couldn't find the words to respond to the man, he was older and wiser and I guess I can see the regret in his eyes; it might be reasonable to give a man willing to change a chance. If I kill him now, I'd be giving the throne to someone like Miran. Though Miran has changed quite a bit, I still wouldn't want to see his capabilities with all that power.

"Be the father, you took from me." I responded; I watched as Marona's face lightened up. It was the closest thing to forgiveness that I could give him. I was actually beginning to look up to Marona as a father figure. Judging from what he said of my father, I think he was a good man; I believe he truly meant for things to happen for the greater good. I shall take the initiative to consider my dads goals, when planning a dream for the future.

Though this doesn't mean I'll be laying down my weapon. Sometimes the world needs a little anarchism, just to keep calm the power hungry giants. I wasn't going to just walk away from Khan; I consider myself to be in the same situation. He should've hurried to kill me, because I'm not ready to show mercy when avenging my brothers. It was a war, and my dream for a brighter future won't come while he continues to live. The Grim Reaper doesn't symbolize death; humans and humans alone symbolize death. Death comes from the chaos that we exhale, what men like Khan live off of.

"Arrun just leave it, lets walk away," suggested Marona. I don't know why he said that. He knew I wouldn't; I guess he was hoping for some change, expecting that the change would come as early as this particular situation. I nodded, to show him that I acknowledged his suggestion. I was still in midst of trying to come to terms with the fact that I'm working with the man that killed my parents; but he seemed to be a lot more freed, a lot more free than I was now of course.

Space was what I needed, sometime alone from this dreaded world I was around on a daily basis. I wanted to be alone, but I know what that does to me; I'd much rather prefer the company of Nilani.

"I'm going to head out now, I need to be alone for a bit," I said.

"Yeah son sure, give me a call if you need anything," responded Marona before opening his arms. I hugged him on the way out; just to assure him that everything was going to be fine.

I tried calling Nilani's phone a few times before I left the Duranji house, but her phone was off. I wasn't surprised; she could possibly be asleep after I kept her up last night. Then again, she's been home for a while, I guess it'd be fine if I go over and pick her up. Besides, she did say that her father wanted to speak to me; I guess I might as well get that over with too.

Chapter 16 – The Collapse

I stepped out of the house to see a familiar face, that of one from my past life. It was Trent, who was one of Hasini's co-workers. I remember meeting him at a work party she once took me to. He was speaking to Miran, curious enough I went over to say hi.

"Trent! What are you doing here?" I asked.

"He's just some reporter; apparently he's working on a story about us," intruded Miran.

"About us?" I questioned.

"Yeah, the Duranji Empire is a force known worldwide, it would make a great story," responded Trent.

"Don't waste your time here bro, you don't want to get involved in this," I suggested.

He seemed to be in a lot of panic, it probably didn't help that Miran was the first person he spoke to.

"You're probably right, I've got to be somewhere else soon. It was good seeing you," responded a rickety Trent.

"So soon? Well if you aren't busy, come by, we'll catch up on a few things," I said.

Miran continued to speak to him, while I began to walk away. Once I got in the car I started having thoughts of the people I left behind. Seeing Trent reminded me that I had another life prior to coming over here. People I left behind, but I guess it was for the best. I'm at the stage where I'm losing people; I wouldn't be able to bear losing a sister or brother due to my actions.

The drive over to Nilani's didn't seem too long, it was nearing 11pm and the traffic had condensed. Upon arriving, I told the security at the front gates that I was here to see Nilani. He was a bit hesitant of letting me in at first, probably because he last saw me holding her at gunpoint, but he received a call to let me in, so he did.

When I rang the doorbell the man at the door responded partially as the Police Commissioner, badgering me with questions.

"Where's Nilani," he asked.

"What do you mean, she came home early in the morning," I responded.

"No she didn't! I've been calling her phone! I thought she was with you!" He shouted.

No, I didn't want to start panicking just yet. I got a text from her saying she got home fine though. Maybe she was with her friend, Dipti. I think that was the name she mentioned yesterday?

"Dipti, do you have her number?" I questioned.

"I've spoke to her already! Nilani isn't with her," he replied in a worrisome tone, curious of her where a bouts. All right I guess it was fine to jump to conclusions now, because Nilani isn't the type of girl to just leave, shutting out the world.

"If anything happens to her because of you," he yelled.

I was starting to fear that Khan maybe behind this, and if that is the case, the tables have truly turned.

"I'll find her!" I said, racing back into the car. I searched for a few hours before parking along side a somewhat busy intersection. I wanted to think that I was just blowing the situation out of hand, and that she may just be busy doing something else, but considering recent events, I couldn't settle on plain hope. I tried calling her phone many times over, hoping she'd pick up.

My last few calls actually had a ring, but she wasn't picking up. Considering that her phone was on I decided to give a call to her father, maybe he'd be able to trace a call if someone picks up or calls.

"Sir, Nilani's phone is on now. Wait for a call and trace it!" I suggested.

He was already on it, but the problem was that we might end up waiting forever on a call that we won't get. I was usually great when it came to coming up with immediate plans, but with it being of Nilani, my mind felt helpless. This is exactly what I was worried about; I knew that letting her in my life would do this. A man's love can turn out to be his biggest weakness, leading to his tragic downfall.

My first love caused my initial downfall; I wasn't prepared to let Nilani's love do the same.

I parked near a street side teashop, and while I had a smoke, I tried sipping down a glass of tea to clear my mind. In the midst of it all I saw Trent, who was carrying a duffle bag, and he did make eye contact with me. Though the response wasn't what I expected, it actually didn't make sense at all. He had that similar panic from earlier today, though I now realized it was towards me, and not Miran! He turned in the opposite direction and attempted to flee. I wasn't slow to respond, I dropped my glass of tea, and ran across the street, holding my right arm out to insure the cars would stop. His heavy bag was slowing him down, and so he tossed it to the side, hopping over a concrete wall I followed. It was a closed out alleyway, eventually he'd meet a dead end, but I caught him much before that.

I tackled him to ground, smacking him against the floor once before picking him up. I then slammed him against the wall; I was bound on figuring out why he was running.

"Why were you running?" I shouted!

"I was late for my bus," he replied, attempting to play it off.

"Don't lie to me you piece of shit," I continued to shout. I didn't plan on wasting my time asking him more questions. I used my left forearm to hold him tight against the alleyway wall, while I bundled him with a few knocks to the face. I let my forearm fall back a bit, and he fell to the floor. He wasn't willing to speak just yet, so I leaned down over him and insured a few more knocks to his head as the blood began to dowse down.

"I'm sorry, I'm sorry," he cried.

"You know! Where is she! Where is Nilani?" I demanded.

"I'm sorry," he repeated.

He was really pushing the wrong buttons, apologizing only made things worse. I was tired of hearing apologies, and he was about to learn it in the worst way possible. He'd probably bleed to death if I continued to smack him across his face, so instead I started to hit him across the body with a long piece of wood I had found on the ground. By the end of it, I knew that I can't expect this guy to speak, but he knew something and that was for sure. I dragged him by his foot, across the street and threw him in the car as people stood aside and watched.

I walked back over to the teashop and asked for another glass of tea, while the few nightwalkers watched in shock. I didn't care for the attention; my thoughts were of what could possibly happen next. Maybe I shouldn't have beaten Trent so hard; he probably knew of Nilani's whereabouts. Though I don't understand what he had to do with it, it makes no sense. Miran said that Trent was just here to cover a story, so why would he have to run from me.

Then it made sense! It was him, it was Trent who was in the car on the bridge; he was the one that slammed me with the metal rod. The white shirt he's wearing resembled that of the masked man! So there's a link; Khan must be linked to Trent in some way! I hate the human mind, we function completely fine until we face a problem; every clear thought becomes a jumble. Though one breaking moment can clear all once again.

I was getting a call; it was from Nilani's phone. I picked up hoping for her voice, and it was.

"Arrun, Arrun!" She cried.

I heard her call out my name twice before I heard Khan's voice. I should've expected this; I should've known that Khan wasn't finished with his antics.

"Arrun? What was the hurry? You should've just made sure that Nilani got home safe! Oh right, right, you had that show to catch right? The one at Napier Bridge, how was that by the way? It was quite a scene, right? This is what happens kid; this is what happens when you try to cross paths with people like me. This game isn't for people who have feelings; just look at you; you must feel so miserable right now. I'm a nice guy though; I won't do anything to harm your girlfriend, but I can't speak for the other guys. They're probably going to beat her, and then pass her around like the piece of trash she is! I want your head, and I'll continue to take the people you care about till I get it. There's no walking away from the game now kid, the only way out is for you to die."

"Khan, I swear to god if you," the line was cut before I could finish. Though if things happen according to plan, Nilani's father should've been able to trace that call. The beep on my phone confirmed of that too; he had been able to trace the call, but the location of her being wasn't so satisfying.

She was apparently held in what was probably one of the most criminally active zones in Chennai. A place where men live lawlessly, and what was worst is that it was one of the spots that backed Khan's activities. It wouldn't be easy to go in there and come out alive, but better me going alone than risking a big riot. The car was already left on idle, and Trent remained unconscious. I expected the Commissioner to be on his way with back up soon, but I wanted to get there and handle the situation prior to his arrival.

I took the wheel, and drove off as the traffic remained still after watching me drag Trent into the car. I was impatient, as I should be; driving as fast as I can, I swerved through the few cars on the road. A few angry drivers, and horning didn't stop my pace and I got near the zone in due time. See the problem was that I forgot my handgun once again. I was left with a machete, and I planned to put it to good use on some of Khans men. Unable to follow my normal guns blazing method I parked the car two blocks out, there was a reduced amount of movement, and it was fairly quiet.

I remained in the car, and waited for brief moment in time as the streets cleared completely. I saw what was a large building, and I if my assumptions were right, Nilani had to be held there!

I stepped out the vehicle and checked around once more before opening the back passenger doors; I wasn't planning on leaving Trent in the car. He's going to serve a purpose, because he's obviously part of something I've yet to find out. It is going to be difficult; right now he's practically dead weight, and caring him the entire way through will be quite hard.

It was exhausting but I dragged him the two-block distance, before throwing him over a fence. The fence gated the tall building, and the back part I laid him at wasn't guarded at all. My initial thoughts were to just walk to the front steps, attacking anyone who tried to stop me, but I should probably try walking in as an ordinary person. I wasn't sure if anyone even knew me, I was actually quite unknown by many here, and it maybe easier to just walk by as an ordinary citizen.

It might be a stupid move, but I tucked the knife between my boxers and pants, and then used my shirt to cover it. I was a bit nervous walking past the sketchy few on the street, but no one recognized me. Once I reached the entrance to the building I realized that it was an unfinished project. Much like most places in the area, really dirty, and probably filled with hazy people.

The man at the front of the building stared at me for a while; I was beginning to think that he maybe knew who I was. I placed my hand on the right side of my hip where I helmed the machete and he began to pace towards me. "How long you staying," he asked. I was quite confused, but he obviously thought that I was here for something else, so I decided to play along.

"Half-hour maybe?" I replied.

"Only? You maybe want to stay for an hour, more worth the money," he continued.

"Sure," I responded, hesitant and unaware of where things were going.

"You seem fairly young, head to the fifth floor. We've got a new girl, she may not want to cooperate because you're the first, but you know what to do."

Yeah, it became fairly obvious as to what sort of things were go on around here. He mentioned a new girl, and it has got to be Nilani. "Follow me," he said as he began to lead the way. We walked up the steps to the entrance, before stepping through the doorway. There wasn't much lighting and the place reeked. There was a counter and room to the left, and stairs leading up on the right. I began to follow the pimp up stairs before another man began to walk down from above. He walked right on by before, asking us to stop.

When we turned his face rang alert, I knew what to expect next so I reacted quick. I pulled the knife quickly before he could act. I first jumped the stairs, and waited for him to react likewise. I had the advantage, holding the machete but I noticed the handgun at his waist. As expected he went for his gun, and it was the best time for me to react. I swiped at his neck and watched him fall, then stuck the machete through his skull.

His blood spattered across my shirt, and when I turned towards the pimp he attempted to flee. I got a hold of his left foot before he could take another step more and dragged him back down the stairs before stabbing him a few times through his chest. This has already become a mess; I noticed a space underneath the stairs that had a door leading outside. It served as an opportunity for me to get Trent in here; I could probably leave him in the room I saw to the left.

After bringing him in, I dragged the two bodies into the room as well. By luck, no one else had made their way down to notice the dead figures. I insured that the door was securely locked before moving back up the stairs. I was on alert most of the way through, but I noticed a man on the steps up to the fifth floor. There was a solid piece of stone I threw to lure him down, and the man who came down was quite old to be a henchman. I ran up on him; like Trent, slammed him against the wall, but used the machete to enlist more fear.

"Where is she? The new girl!" I demanded.

"Next floor above, last room on the left!" He cried, trembling upon seeing the knife forced to his neck. I used the handle part of the machete to knock him unconscious before racing up the next flight of steps. I really don't know why that man was standing there, but the fifth floor was empty much like the others. I was expecting a lot more of Khans men to be watching the premises. Walking cautiously down the narrow hallway I reached the last room on the left without being caught. You could hear the cry of woman inside, and when I opened the door tied and placed in the corner was not Nilani.

"Don't come closer, please leave me alone!" Cried the girl.

"Look, I'm not going to do anything to you," I said.

"Please, show me mercy. I'm not that type of girl." She begged.

I walked closer, and with every step I took she yearned to be left alone. I placed the knife on the ground, and continued to walk closer. I kneeled down beside her, and she was drenched in tears.

"Please let me go, I don't belong here. Please!" She continued.

"I'll take you home, where do you need to go," I inquired.

"Toronto, Canada," She said.

"Toronto? How on Earth did you end up here?" I asked.

"They kidnapped us, I'm not the only one. There are so many more girls like me. These men are monsters; they keep us all at a house next to this property, for months we've been hoping for a way out. They're using us as sex slaves, who gave them the right to determine our lives? I was a med school student, and now I'm here. Some of the girls have even leaped over the top of this building after they get raped. While the rest of us remained in that house, praying that we won't be next. Some of the girls have just given in, and they're just miserable. They can't speak, they've been beaten, they're practically used till they serve no purpose;

its completely gruesome. Please, help me"

"What's your name?" I questioned.

"Sarah," She replied.

"Sarah, that's my mothers name. Think of me as your brother, you and all the girls will get home," I reassured.

I could tell she felt relieved of sort, kind of like her prayers had been answered. She smiled in the midst of tears, but I still had no clue of where Nilani might be. Perhaps that's why this building was empty of Khan's men. Maybe Nilani was in the same house, among those other girls, praying for me to come get her.

"When did they bring you here from that house," I inquired.

"It's probably been about half an hour," presumed Sarah.

"Was there a new girl? One that was brought in earlier today?" I questioned.

"It's you, you're Arrun! She kept saying you'd come!" She replied.

"How is she? Is she fine?" I asked.

"They were kind of aggressive when they brought her in, but she's fine," said Sarah.

There it was, finally the break in my head, I form of relief. It was enough to know that she was fine, but it was another thing to be able to save her. It was going to be much harder, trying to facilitate through a house to get Nilani. It would be more compact and there would be more men for me to take out in a certain space. She was going to come home with me though, that was one thing I was set on.

I untied Sarah, and picked up the machete before asking her to follow me. We eased back down the stairs, right back to the sketchy street; there seemed to be more attention on us, though this time I didn't hide the knife. They saw the blood on the machete, how it matched that of my shirt and hands. I continued to walk in direction of the house next to the building, scratching the machete against the floor beneath us. I was hoping for Khan to hear the scratching, as I did after he slashed my friend.

While a few stared at the sides of the street, two men were present the entrance. They knew exactly who I was, they didn't hesitate a second before running towards me. I stopped and waited for them to cover half the distance between us. Once they reached the half waypoint, I ran up towards them as well. They both carried knives, like mine; and when they swung I dropped to the ground as they missed. Though I didn't, I insured to make a cut on one of their legs, the man on the right was the easiest to catch. Once he dropped to the floor, I was left having to deal with the other. After running past me he stood in front of Sarah, I thought he'd maybe use her as a method of killing me so I decided to draw more attention towards me.

Smacking the machete against the ground I shouted, "Do something, you piece of shit!"

There was one certain thing about men; many of us don't have the capability to think twice. Especially when it comes to insults being thrown at one another, we act off instincts, and that's what he did.

He came at me once more I was able to dodge his first attempt, but he got me on another. A slice over my left shoulder, I fell back a little and swung my knife upwards through his abdomen. Once he dropped, I insured that the both of them were dead. I then told Sarah to continue following me.

"You're bleeding," she said.

"I know, don't worry about it, keep following me," I replied.

She walked behind every step I took, and she pointed me in the direction I should walk. I wasn't looking forward to crossing the third man; he was huge! He was a bit slow to notice me, his back was turned the other way, and I saw it as an opportunity.

"Hey, fat slob!" I shouted.

He was slow to turn, and the moment he did I hove the machete straight through his abdomen. Yet, he stood; looking straight down on me he kicked me right down. I felt the sharp pain through my chest, but the stab was doing its job. He was acting slowly, and I gained the strength to get back up. I ran to find more strength and drop kicked him to the floor before pulling the machete out. Then, I slammed it once more through his chest. That was the end of that, and to my luck his revolver had fallen to the ground. I left the machete on the ground and picked it up instead, something I've grown a bit comfortable using. The big ogre was blocking the doorway that was supposed to lead us to the captive girls. Sarah helped me roll him over before we walked down the steps.

"Khaj?" Spoke a voice; I guess the big ogre's name was Khaj. I'm pretty sure they heard the big thump to the floor when he fell, and so they were going to be prepared. We remained at the top of the steps.

"Sarah, I think we should roll this guy down the stairs. Help me out," I said.

I assumed that we could use Khaj as a distraction of sorts. It was hard, but we managed to roll the fat slob down the steps. We waited, and the men that remained downstairs did the same. I made Sarah wait behind the wall to insure her safety; I remained in a prone stance atop the steps. It took sometime, but I could hear the footsteps of a man walking slowly towards Khaj's body. He walked with his foot dragging against the floor; he let me know exactly where he was with every step he took. A sudden bang, he fired a shot. It just missed me; I guess he tried to fire it for assurance. He slipped though, because he didn't fire a second bullet fast enough. He made himself vulnerable, and I saw it work to my advantage. Sarah remained upstairs, and after the man fell to the floor I took quiet steps down the stair.

I could hear the whispers of two men; there was no hope of picking up Khaj's body so I used that of the second mans as a shield. It was obvious that the remaining men had not seen me; if they had I would've been gunned down by now. I took the body of the man and threw it in front of me, and just as I assumed bullets were fired. I waited for their clip to be emptied before I walked out. I shot down a first man on the left, while the second was having some difficulty reloading his gun. I began walking in his direction and he probably assumed that it would be smarter to just rush me. Though we both knew that he wouldn't win, I gunned him down as well, and he fell straight down to my feet. Now all that remained were a few dead bodies, and a door on the left of a dark basement.

"Sarah, you can come down now!" I shouted.

She came down, shocked and shivering she pointed to the door on the left.

"That's where the girls should be," she said.

I tried to yank the door, but it wouldn't budge. It was locked from the outside, and I'm pretty sure that one of these bodies lying around must have had the key. Sarah began checking the bodies of the men, but I noticed how scared she was.

"Sarah, don't worry about it. I'll find the key," I said.

She smiled and waited on the side, as I flipped through the bloody mess I caused. Khaj helmed the key at his waist, and when I placed the key in the whole and turned it in the right direction I took a deep breath. I could be walking into a trap, it wasn't easy at all to get passed those few men, but there really was a possibility of more waiting beyond the door; considering the fact that I hadn't heard a single voice in reaction to all the gun shots being fired.

Running in Sarah cried, hugging the other women. I was breath taken, I was in disbelief; I couldn't believe the amount of women that were being held captive in such a small space.

"Arrun!" Screamed a voice.

Nilani, she came rushing towards me, relief. I didn't care about anything in the world, she was fine and that mattered enough to me. Nilani held on to me tight, and all the captivated women came and circled us. It felt amazing; they were all filled with tears of relief. I felt like I gave them hopes of a safe passage home, but there was still one unfinished business.

"You're bleeding Arrun," said Nilani.

"Where is he," I asked.

There he was at the corner of my eyes, trying to sneak through the side.

"Khan!" I shouted.

There it was, the fear, it was in his eyes again. Where'd all that tough talk of his go? Where were my friends? Dead, they were dead; he had to beg. I wanted him to beg for his life.

"Get on your knees," I ordered.

"Fear it's a beautiful thing isn't it. It comes to terrorize, and in a spark of a moment you think you have control over it. Though it will return. It does return, doesn't it? Isn't it fear in your eyes right now? You should've felt the fear of my presence when cutting Thambi piece for piece. You should've known the fear of your future when you made me watch as you sliced Remone's neck before my eyes. The barrel in the revolver has one bullet left. Lets give it a spin, and see how lucky you get. Three shots, if you withstand it all I 'll let you walk away."

"Please," he begged.

"One shot, I guess you're a little lucky today," I said.

"Two, damn you must have done something great in your life," I continued.

"Sorry, I'm Sorry! I'll walk away, from everything!" Khan cried.

"Three! Well then, I guess you deserve to walk free. Get up!" I ordered.

We both knew he wouldn't get to walk; I mean wouldn't you kill the devils minions if you had the chance. Shaken with lost hope he got up off of his knees, and tears drenched down his face.

"Some men don't deserve the blessing of tears," I said.

The barrel emptied, and as his blood splatted across my chest, you could hear the piercing of a bullet going through his skull, but it was finally over. No respect was shown, some of the women even spit on his dead body.

Chapter 17 – Commencement

I left back my blood stained red shirt, and walk out with the black t-shirt I wore underneath. Whipped the revolver clean, and placed it in Khan's hands before wiping the machete and hiding it behind my shirt. When I walked out of the house with say forty plus captive girls, a large crowd had begun to form. The Commissioner and his men had just made their way there, and he was glad to know that Nilani was safe.

I guess he didn't want to step down; he simply gave me a nod to acknowledge my actions. After speaking to her father, Nilani came back to my side. She was insisting that we head over to a hospital, or at least the standby paramedics on site. Though there remained one person to take out of the picture. One thing was certain; Trent had to be working with Khan, and with him out of the picture, there was no purpose that Trent served.

Nilani followed me as I headed into the building I first searched. He was awake by the time I got back; I could hear the banging on the door.

"Where are you going Arrun," asked Nilani.

"Unfinished business," I replied.

"Arrun, leave it. Khan's dead; there's no point anymore." She said.

"No lose ends, I'm not watching anyone else get hurt!" I shouted.

She knew that there would be no purpose in continuing to argue. She simply followed and watched as I opened the door. Trent was stunned; he fell back to the ground and attempted to crawl backwards. Nilani didn't want to watch, but I guess she understood.

"I'm sorry," he cried.

It's seemed as if that's all he's been doing, apologizing. I wasn't going to feel bad about this; in fact if there were one thing I learned, it would be to never spare a man that has a negative impact on the lives of innocent souls. He pushed his arms out and covered his head when I swung out the machete. I crowned it in the air and just when I was about to force it upon his life I heard a scream. Sarah was at the door, with her hand covering her mouth.

"It was him! He was there," She screamed; the chill in her voice was evident.

"Where?" I questioned.

"He was with that other man, the one that brought us all here," she replied.

"They drowned that journalist girl; he was there," she continued.

Twisted, that's what I felt. Twisted in thoughts that shouldn't have been raised.

"Who's she talking about Trent," I asked.

"I'm sorry, I'm sorry," he repeated.

I smacked him across his already bruised face once more.

"Hasini! It was Hasini!" He cried.

There it was, the answer I didn't want to hear. The machete dropped to the floor, as I did too. As tears began to drench down my cheek, I realized that I mourned the wrong death. It changed everything, it wasn't the way things were supposed to play out; Hasini was taken away from me. A blank mental state, I didn't know what to do. I remembered it again; I remember her face as she laid covered by the white cloth. I remember crying for her to return; I didn't need to be here, she didn't need to be dead.

"Who was it? Who was the other man you piece of shit! Who was it?" I shouted.

"Miran." He replied.

Shame on me, I called him my brother. How could I be so naive? I knew the type of the person he is; yet I gave him another chance. He is responsible for the death of the woman I loved. The woman that taught me to love, the one I pictured being the mother of my children, and at one point or another laying at my side while I'm on my deathbed.

Instead he was the only one responsible for the treachery I inhibited trying to forget what once was, what she was.

"Did she cry?" I asked.

"Did she beg?" I continued.

"Did he hit her?" I urged.

"I'm sorry," he replied.

"Sorry, sorry, sorry! That's all you've been saying. Do you think that'll save you? You guys took her from me! Why'd you do that, she saw you as a friend. Do you have any clue of how many good things she has told me about you?"

I didn't waste another second before I picked up the machete again. I swung it up and down with force, multiply. I couldn't stop; I didn't know what got into me. It was something beyond anger and rage. His blood spattered all across the floor, and his limbs were breaking free and yet I couldn't stop. I continued to slash him till I felt the pressure of Nilani pulling me back. Drenched in blood, tamed by grief I sat down against the wall and just cried.

"Nilani, they took her from me," I cried.

"She didn't need to die," I continued.

"Where was I? I bet she cried out for me, and I couldn't do anything." I shouted.

"Arrun, kill him," she said.

I glanced back up at her, and she wiped the tears off my face. I know how much she meant to you, and she didn't deserve to die the way she did.

> "I don't know if I want to support all the crimes you've committed, but Miran deserves to die a cruel death. Don't let him get into your head, be the strong man that I love. Don't harm yourself asking irrational questions; surely you would've gone to help her if you had known the

situation she was in. You fought the odds to find me, and that's an indication of how strong your power to love is. Finish it Arrun, end it all, and give this place a new beginning."

She was right, but in those moments I felt miserable. I couldn't spark my mentality reckless enough to fuel vengeance. I continued to cry; both Nilani and Sarah helped me walk out the building and outside stood my men. I failed to consider whether they knew of Hasini or not. Marona was the first to catch my attention, and I his; he walked towards me and I was boiled with mixed emotions.

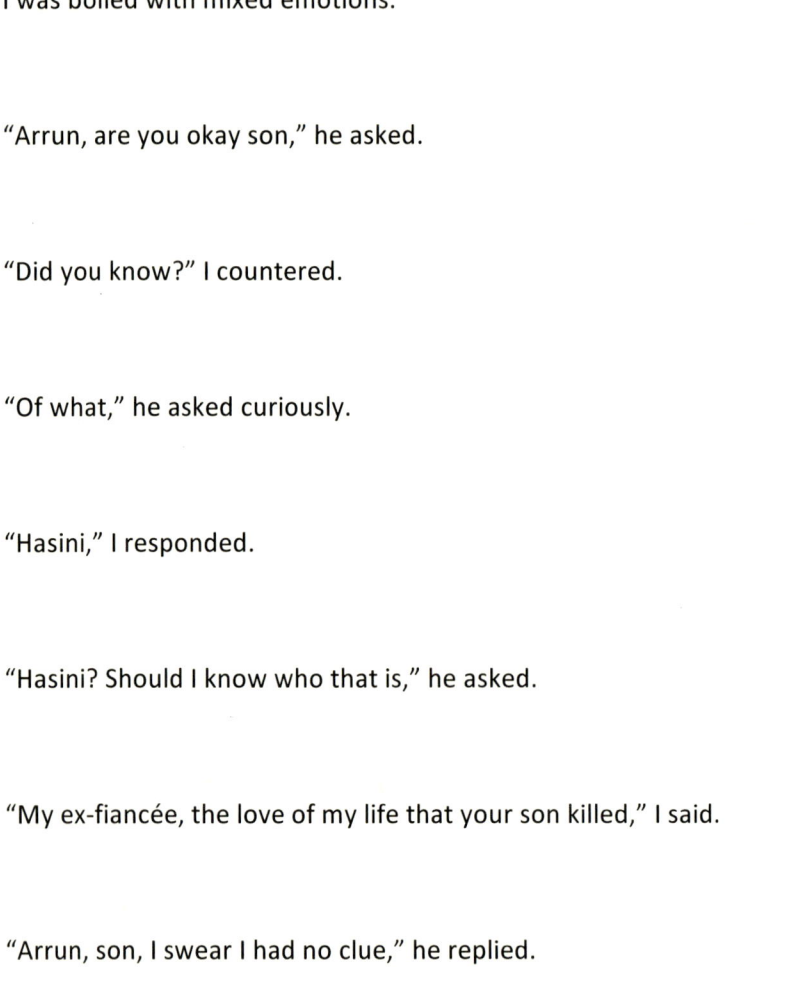

"Arrun, are you okay son," he asked.

"Did you know?" I countered.

"Of what," he asked curiously.

"Hasini," I responded.

"Hasini? Should I know who that is," he asked.

"My ex-fiancée, the love of my life that your son killed," I said.

"Arrun, son, I swear I had no clue," he replied.

"Yeah, bet you didn't know that he was working with Khan either!" I shouted.

"Where the fuck is he?" I shouted, as the rage finally began showing its form.

Most of them stood in shock at my accusations, like they didn't want to believe it. Though things started to make sense; Khan had always seemed to figure out our whereabouts, Miran wasn't acceptant of my arrival at first, and from what the guys say he hasn't been home since I saw him speaking to Trent. I was furious, and I yearned to drench myself in his blood.

I felt it tearing apart, my mentality was beginning to snap; Nilani's grip against my arm didn't favor a thing either. I turned, looking deep into her eyes, and I knew I should walk away. It was best for her; my actions, my surroundings will kill her. With trembling hands I took grasp of her fingers holding tight against my arm, and pulled apart.

"Walk away," I said.

"Arrun, I could stay," she replied.

"Not just now, don't come back," I continued.

"Do you know what you're asking of me," she asked.

"Please," I pleaded.

"Arrun, don't do this now. You don't want to," she said.

"Just get out of my face, this isn't your fate," I said.

"Arrun." She cried.

"Leave!" I shouted.

I knew that I was hurting her, the tears made it evident. I held back mines and walked away. I had a bigger plan in mind; all my focus was set on finding Miran. I looked back, I really do love her, but her well being had to be my priority. When her father began walking her to the car, she kept calling out my name, but I turned away and didn't look back. That's the secret in turning back, you can't look back to truly walk away.

"She loves you man, don't leave her like that," said Verone.

"You think I don't? She's better off without me, she'll realize it," I replied.

"Please, lets just figure where Miran is. Will you help me?" I asked.

"You're more of a brother than he ever was, of course I will," replied Verone.

Everyone stood around me. Marona, Verone, Renny, Sethu, and all other friends; except one. One who silently walked away, thinking he'd be unnoticed. He was looking really suspicious, and I had a doubt in the way he spoke on the phone. I figured he'd be talking Miran; Jeremy was one among the house who shared a close bound with Miran. They've known each other through their childhood, and he must've been filling him in on our next move. As the others tried consoling me, I remained keen on keeping my eyes on Jeremy, waiting for him to cut the line.

Eventually he did, I shoved aside both Renny and Sethu before walking towards Jeremy.

"Where is he," I asked.

"Who? Bro you're bleeding!" He replied.

"Cut the bullshit, where's Miran?" I shouted.

Everyone started noticing our conversation on the side, and began walking forth.

"What's the problem here?" Asked Marona.

"This trash right here knows where Miran is!" I shouted.

"Is that true Jeremy, do you know where his," asked Verone.

"I swear I don't, I was just calling home," He replied.

"Check his phone," I suggested.

He showed retaliation, and that moment alone proved his guilt. I acted off instincts and hit with force across the face. Once he fell to the ground I kept beating him, until an officer on scene came rushing towards us.

"Stand down officer," ordered Marona.

The officer, or any officer for that case really had no voice in this part of the world. He couldn't help but walk away, revolting would've just left him dead; at least he was smart. Something Jeremy wasn't; he remained quiet, loyalty at his finest.

"I'm going to dial Miran's number, keep it on speaker, and you're going to ask where he is," I said.

We stood around as the ring went through, and when Miran answered, Jeremy did as ordered. All to the point where he tried to flee.

"They know where you are Miran! Leave!" Shouted Jeremy.

That was the death of him; Sethu smoked him with a bullet and didn't thinking twice about it. There really wasn't a purpose for him to serve, and his loyalty to Miran would've eventually led me to kill him anyhow, so no one really showed any care. Miran was supposedly at some girl's house, the house of a widowed woman he's been seeing for sometime now.

"Call our guys in the area, and ask if they've seen Miran," I instructed; Sethu walked away to the corner in response to my orders and began making calls. Verone stood beside me and urged for me to get some medical attention, I tried deny the request, but I was actually starting to bleed out quite hard. There was an ambulance that remained on scene, and they helped get my stiches done. All the while I forgot that Sarah and the other girls were still present. The time was nearing 6am, and the media started rolling in, and as I assumed they eventually started shedding light on my face.

"Are you done yet," I asked.

"One second...done," replied the paramedic.

That was my queue to walk away; I really wasn't ready for the camera's to start capturing my face. I shoved them to the side as I got into the car with Verone.

"I know a place we could go Arrun, it'll help, trust me," said Verone, trying to keep my mind of things. I really don't think any place in the world would make me feel at ease right now, but he was holding the ashes of Remone at his side, so I sat quietly as he drove.

~

We drove out an hour before reaching a view only the birds, and blessed ones may see. Verone handed me Remone's ashes and stepped out the vehicle.

"Come out," he waved.

As beautiful as the view may be, the thought of Hasini's murderer being out there, alive, is still bugging me. As it should; to be completely honest I had no clue of whom I can trust anymore. I mean I went about thinking these past few days that I had found a new family, but there laid a quiet black sheep who is responsible for the soul depression in my life. I was able to forgive Marona; I mean I think I did, though it was certain that there was no forgiveness in sights for Miran. I stood beside Verone, and I was hesitant. He brought me to a really quiet place, the type of place where you'd kill someone.

"You don't trust us anymore, do you," asked Verone; It's as if he read my mind.

"No it's not that," I said.

"There's no reason to lie, I would think the same," replied Verone.

"Though I really brought you here because this is a place Remone loved," he said.

"Really, he's never brought me here," I replied.

"I'm sure he would've sooner or later," claimed Verone; I didn't know where he was going with this, but I listened.

"Remone was about nineteen when I first brought him here. Just a kid, scared of what his life will come of. I saw him to be more of a sibling to me; I considered Remone as god's gift to me. When I first saw him he was getting beat by some of our men, I didn't see a single tear in the kids eyes, but the first time I brought him here; he cried like a heart broken girl. One thing is for sure, he had a rough childhood, and he

earned the right to let out that heartache. I let him cry to his hearts content that day, and you see the view of Chennai you see out there; I asked him to take a deep look into it. He stopped his tears and asked me why I wanted him to do so. I told him to forget the world that hurt him, leave the past behind, instead to prepare himself for the world he'll be taming. He said he wanted to be like me. I didn't understand why he'd want to be like me, but his answer was that I wasn't a monster. He saw me to be something none other would consider. He saw me to be something else, and I don't know if I lived up to what he thought of me, but I want to. I see it in you Arrun, you can help me be the idol he saw in me."

"He loved you Verone, I could say that much," I said.

"I know, but I want you to be the one to conduct his last rites, I know he'd want you to do it," said Verone. I was quite hesitant, I thought Verone should be the one do so, but he insisted of me to do it. Holding the urn of Remone's ashes I remembered the first time I ever spoke to him. I remember barking at him for being hesitant of selling me marijuana; thinking I was an undercover officer or something.

I felt a break within myself when I walked over to the edge of the cliff; I looked upon the view of Chennai and let the ashes run through the wind. It almost felt as if Remone was present amongst us. I only pray for the souls of both Thambi and Remone to be at peace.

"We should get going," Verone suggested; I took a final glance of the view, and vowed upon myself to make sure the city runs as beautiful as it seems from up here.

We got in the car and drove off, but on the way back to the Duranji residence I received calls from Renny, Sethu, and a few others of Miran's whereabouts; all of them ended up being negative responses. I felt a brief moment of peace atop that cliff, but once my head returned to the situation at hand everything changed. The urge for vengeance steamed to be priority. I noticed Verone feeling my vibe; he didn't speak a word till we reached the house.

"We'll get him don't worry," he consoled. It was shocking to see the amount of support I was receiving from the guys. I expected a lot of hostility after wanting to kill Miran, but I guess no one respects a traitor, even if they share the bond of family.

"He's also responsible for Remone and Thambi's death, I remember that," he continued. Marona was waiting for us at the front steps of the house, curious to know if we had word of Miran. To be honest I had mixed opinions as to where he stood on the circumstances, I mean we are after his son. Though a man as reckless as him probably wouldn't care for the bond of family, after all he didn't care when he killed my father.

"Verone, stay here. Arrun, let's swing by Raja's place. I want to see if he's okay," said Marona. I was desperate to find Miran, and if it meant searching the world, I was ready. I nodded and took the driver seat in the vehicle. Through the ride he continued speaking in my favor; though he did mention that he had never thought Miran would stoop so low to turn against family.

I opened the door, and there he was. Miran! Leaving out the front door of Raja's house. My immediate reaction was to pull out the handgun and fire at will, and Marona did the same, but we missed. Miran ran back into the house, and I after him. I rushed through the front door, and bam! Miran missed my head by an inch, as the bullet graced the side of the wall. Near death? Who cares, I raced right behind him. He ran out the back entrance and ran straight for the back wall. Marona fired a few shots at Miran from outside, but they all missed wide.

He had the head start; I jumped and held myself up against the wall to see how far he had gotten before rushing back to the car.

"Get Raja, one of his cars, and follow!" I shouted, as Marona looked upon in shock. He was too old and slow for me to drag along. I raced back into reverse and drove around the street to catch up to Miran. Turning right, I watched him pull aside an on coming driver. I shot the gun in the air, but it worked in his favor. The driver of the oncoming vehicle fled the vehicle in fear. Before getting into the car he gave me a smirk.

Both vehicles stood head to head, like two angry bulls. The engines roared, and we speared for one another. Both cars were on the verge of being totaled, and that meant the driver too. I was ready, but Miran wasn't. He made a quick move to the right before both vehicles met. I got him nice though, a hit to the left rear bumper and both cars met side by side. We both fired shots, but missed. After the first shot was fired, Miran jetted in the direction he initially headed.

I followed recklessly, firing shots in hopes of getting him, but I trailed with no luck. Though I didn't show any less of a fight, I chased him with a minimal break in space. I raced behind him through the residential premises, but we soon entered the busy streets of Chennai. A lot harder to drive in, especially considering the speed we were going at.

We raced through as an audience gathered, and in the midst of the citizens running was a little girl. I slammed the break hard enough to stop, but I failed to notice the on coming traffic. The impact to the left of the vehicle caused a flip, and there it went. The car was flipped upside down, as I attempted to crawl out. The stinging ring in my ear only made things worse for a blurry vision.

I attempted to snap out of it, and it took some time but I noticed that my stiches had opened up. A few scars and cuts but I should be fine, or so I think. When I finally got out, I leaned against the car. My ears were still ringing, and things still felt a bit fuzzy, but I noticed a girl jumping and waving her arms. I was in the midst of turning in the direction, and pop! I was stricken down with a menacing hit to my jaw; I shook out the feeling once more but I wasn't pleased to see Miran in power.

He hailed over me, holding me by my shirt, knocking me continuously to the face. The pain was excruciating, and I witnessed the blood drip relentlessly to the ground. For the first time since I've arrived in Chennai, I was presented as the victim to the crowd gathered. I felt so weak, not because of my physical state, but because I was failing my lost ones. I needed to be the one pounding Miran; I should've seen the end of him for killing Hasini. The crowd watched, and not a single soul stepped forward to help. Nor did I expect them to; I wasn't part of a single act to earn their love.

"C'mon hero! Where'd all that toughness go now? You were really dumb enough to think that I'd consider you a brother? I don't even consider Verone a brother, let alone a weak trash like you from Toronto. This is where you end up, when you cross paths with the kingpin of the underworld. My father? He's old, and his time is most certainly up. I'm tired of listening to that old mans orders; Miran do this, Miran do that. It's fucking bullshit! Yes, I'm the one that hired a man to take him out in Toronto. Yes, I'm the one who has been helping Khan know where every single one of our men are at all times. The incident when you first arrived, the brothel situation, I even let them know where Remone and Thambi were. Oh I heard the screams Thambi made when they cut him piece by piece; it was just symphonic. This is what happens when you cross my path; you could even ask, what was her name, Hasini? She was such a saint wasn't she, trying to save people in my parts of the world. Oh, the way she begged and cried to be freed. Don't worry "brother" you'll be with your friends in the after life soon enough."

I felt miserable; I couldn't bear hearing the things he had to say. The worst of it all, is the feeling of death creeping the atmospheres. I was getting tired of running away from death. Maybe this it, maybe my end means life for my loved ones. Though the scorching energy of the sun didn't give up on me. It's radiant heat burned through the cuts on my face, waking me, bringing life within me once more. Miran walked back to the car; my guess, to probably get his gun. I saw it as a chance; I remained on the ground, but swiftly swiped a shattered piece of glass in my hand.

A bit late but on time, arrived the rest of the guys.

"Miran, don't do anything you'll regret," warned Verone. Taking his handgun out of the vehicle, Miran paced towards Verone and the others. Walking right passed me he pointed the gun in their direction. I turned around, looked directly at my men and waived my head side to side. They knew to stand down, but no one knew of what Miran was thinking.

"Oh big brother, you know, you should be standing at my side. This empire will be ours. You, Raja, and me; we'll run an empire like no other! Yes dad, you're trusted friend Raja has been with me from the beginning. I thought I'd be safe at his house. Who would've thought you two would come storming in all the sudden. Raja, you might as well come stand at my side now, how long can you stay attached to the weakest link."

Raja walked as asked, and stood side by side with Miran. While in the back, storming with the remaining energy I surged myself to my feet. Walked behind Miran and turned him to my face before diving the piece of glass through his chest. Utter shock, is what I saw in his eyes. He failed to know that the weak man on the ground would always surge to his heights when given the time.

On his knees he remained, eyes wide opened, awaiting his sentence. With the public to witness, I picked up Miran's gun and drilled a bullet straight through his head. No speech, not a word; just a message. I didn't wait a second more before shooting a bullet through both of Raja's knees. His screams could wake the dead, and so on that note I called forth Verone and Marona. The clip was empty on the handgun, and so with a drop of tear, Verone handed me his gun. Bam! Bam! There went both knees of Marona too. Screaming in pain, his tearing soul had no answer, no explanations.

"I'm sorry dad, it is necessary for the greater good," said Verone. Verone didn't wish to take part; it was part of the deal.

~

I only pray for the souls of both Thambi and Remone to be at peace. I continued to stare out into the graveyard Chennai has become. Verone stood at my side, and I was pretty certain that he was having a battle of the mind, the worst kind of war.

"Stand with me for a better future, one that'll allow you to live even after death. To live beyond death you need to capture the hearts of the innocent, and with our stat sheet it won't be easy if we remain the same. Drastic changes are necessary; what I'm about to suggest may not set easy with you, but it has to be done. Just stand with my opinion, and the rest will prove to be for the best."

"What do you have in mind," asked Verone.

"Miran alone wont fixed this problem. The death of Marona and Raja is mandatory. It has to be done to end a dreaded chapter. I won't ask you to do it, but stand with my plan. We'll walk away; use our power to enforce the well being of the helpless civilians. This is the better person you could be Verone."

"Understood," responded Verone in acceptance to my proposal.

I was glad to see his acceptance, knowing it was a tough task. I turned away from Verone and continued to gaze upon the rebuild of a kingdom.

"We should get going," suggested Verone.

~

Verone walked back into the crowd, and now I had center stage to make my voice heard. With time meeting it's end, I felt at peace staring at the dead body of Miran. A pleasure of sorts, though I insured that Marona and Raja got my undivided attention. I drenched my hands with the blood off my face, and wiped it on the both their shirts.

"That's the blood of my father, a man capable of forgiving," I started.

> "How unfortunate for you both, I may not be as kind as assumed. Marona, I honestly did see of you as a father, and to you I was a son I assume. Though at the end of the day that too is a lie. A world maybe built on lies, but a functional world cannot be a lie. The life you promise me will be a lie, unless I act accordingly. I want you to stare out into the crowd. The mass crowd of blameless people you've slaved and leeched off of for decades. I want you to beg for their forgiveness, and if they do

forgive you, you will be spared. Beg!"

Marona lived to his name; the moment I asked him to beg, he sucked up all the pain and remained speechless. Raja on the other hand whom was helpless, weak, and unworthy of life begged for forgiveness. It was quite depressing; no one came to his aid. Bang! The moment he dropped, I looked out in to the crowd of watchers.

Amongst the crowd, I saw tears, I saw smiles, and I saw liberation, preparing to break free.

"Marona, Marona, Marona. You're surely a man of your image aren't you? So much pride, what shall we do with it. Why don't we dismantle it?"

"You! Kid in the black shirt, and khaki pants. Come here," I ordered. Nervous, shaking to the bone walked forth a young boy. Probably seventeen years old in age scared of what might happen to him.

"Spit on this guys face," I demanded, yanking back Marona's head. The kid was scared, and I didn't want him to be. He needed a little push.

"Kid look me in my eyes! Men like this guy right here are responsible for the fear you feel. You're a young man, strong, powering, and a leader of the future. You cannot be scared of people who abuse their power! Men like him are responsible for the deaths of parents, leaving children like you orphaned and alone! Men like him are responsible for the rapes of

woman, woman that are scared to look at themselves in the mirror, because they're unable to remember how beautiful they are! Men like him are responsible for the hardships in the lives of every single person in this crowd right now. Now spit!"

Hawking back, the kid gave Marona a nasty one to the face, and smiled up at me with great satisfaction. It caught on, I held his head back as men would come and give him a punch to the face. Woman would take off their slipper and slap him across the face. Children even came by and urinated in front of him. I let it go for a bit, and when I asked them to stop, they did. This time around I saw the liberation in the eyes of almost every individual standing in the crowd. Liberation from a world they were oppressed by, an independence day of the new century.

Letting go of his hair, you could see the life just drained out of him. A man left without his biggest asset, pride. I stood a meter away from him and watched as his head hung low in shame.

"You see Marona, you thought you had it all. You thought you had them all controlled. You helmed your pride so high, but where is it now? Why has your head fallen so short? You see this is it, a snap second. It's all that it takes, to change the story of a life, and yours ends right here."

Gun to the floor, the crowd roared in acceptance. A crowd symbolizing a new found family, and among them a heartbroken love. I stood bloodied and transformed; within the midst of my next crossroad, I rose to be the king of my domain.